LOST IN SALES

A HILARIOUS JOURNEY THROUGH TARGETS AND TRIBULATIONS

ADITYA KUMAR

Made with ♥ on the Notion Press Platform
www.notionpress.com

Contents

Contents

Foreword

Writing a book is always challenging. It's a journey filled with moments of inspiration, frustration, and everything in between. After completing my first book, "The Developmentwala," I found myself in that peculiar space where the desire to create something new clashed with the emptiness of a blank page.

However, as fate would have it, a casual conversation with a dear friend changed everything. Amidst congratulatory remarks for my previous work, he jokingly suggested that I pen down our adventures in the corporate world. Little did I know that seemingly innocuous suggestion would spark the genesis of this book.

Fifteen years ago, we were fresh-faced novices navigating the labyrinthine streets of Mumbai's corporate jungle. Our misadventures, trials, and triumphs in that cutthroat world of sales and bottom lines became the fodder for this narrative.

This book is not just about recounting those days; it's about reliving them, capturing the essence of camaraderie, resilience, and the indomitable spirit that propelled us forward. It's a tribute to all those who, like us, embarked on their professional journeys armed with naivety and ambition.

Happy reading!
Aditya Kumar
www.adityaspire.com

1
The Beginning

Arjun's hands fidgeted with the frayed edges of his worn-out shirt, starkly contrasting the meticulously groomed appearance he usually maintained for his previous job interviews. With each passing minute, his frustration grew, and the thought of presenting himself immaculately for yet another interview felt like an unbearable burden. "What's the point?" he muttered, resigning himself to his disheveled appearance.

It was the 35th organization that had come for placements at their college, marking the end of the line for Arjun and his fellow students. Most of his peers had already secured coveted positions, leaving Arjun with a sinking feeling that this might be his last chance to land a job before graduation.

As the wait stretched, his patience wore thin, and he made a rash decision to retreat to his room. Exhausted and defeated, he returned to his hostel room and collapsed onto his bed, not bothering to change his wrinkled attire. Sleep enveloped him like a heavy blanket, offering a temporary escape from the turmoil of his thoughts.

Moments later, his phone pierced the silence of his room, jolting him awake. "Hello?" he mumbled groggily, still half-asleep.

"Arjun, you won't believe it! You've been selected!" Abhijit's voice crackled with excitement on the other end of the line.

"Come on, dude! Give me a break! Today is not the right time to pull my leg. I am depressed!" He rubbed his eyes, yawning and trying to ignore Abhijit.

"Buddy! I am not joking! I am standing right in front of the notice board, and your name is at the top of the list of selected students!"

Arjun's eyes shot open in disbelief, his drowsiness evaporating instantly. "What? Are you serious?" he exclaimed, his heart pounding with a mixture of disbelief and joy.

"I'm dead serious, man! Get back here quick!" Abhijit urged, his excitement palpable even through the phone.

Arjun leaped out of bed with a newfound burst of energy and raced back to the interview room, his earlier weariness forgotten in the face of this unexpected turn of events. As he scanned the notice board, a surge of elation washed over him as he spotted his name among the chosen few.

A wide grin spread across his face as he realized that, despite the odds, he had succeeded. As he embraced Abhijit in a jubilant hug, he knew that this victory was not just his alone—it was a testament to resilience, perseverance, and the unwavering support of friends who believed in him even when he doubted himself.

"Go on! They have asked all selected candidates to assemble in the interview hall."

As Arjun and the other eight selected candidates gathered in the interview hall, anticipation hung thick in the air. Their nerves had calmed down and they were joyous. Their faces were cheery and had a glint in their eyes.

The HR executive from the company who had interviewed Arjun abruptly stood up, a mischievous gleam in his eyes. "Alright, folks, time for the final round: a group discussion to decide who will be chosen for the job!" he declared, causing a collective wave of panic to ripple through the room. Arjun's stomach churned as he exchanged nervous glances with the other candidates.

But just as they were all on the verge of hyperventilating, the HR executive burst into laughter, the sound echoing through the room like a relieving symphony. "Just kidding, folks! You should've seen the looks on your faces!" he chuckled, wiping away tears of mirth from his eyes.

As the tension dissolved into relieved laughter, the HR executive cleared his throat, his expression sobering. "Alright, now that we've got that out of the way, I want to take a moment to welcome each and every one of you to our company," he began, his voice tinged with sincerity.

He delivered a heartfelt speech about the company's values, goals, and expectations, painting a vivid picture of the challenges and opportunities ahead. He emphasized the importance of hard work, dedication, and adaptability, especially in the fast-paced world of sales.

"In this role, you'll be tasked with selling insurance, a job that comes with its own unique set of challenges," the HR executive continued, his tone grave. "But I have every confidence that you have what it takes to succeed. And remember, we're here to support you every step of the way."

As the speech drew to a close, the HR executive extended his hand to each candidate, his smile warm and welcoming. "Congratulations once again, and welcome aboard. I wish you all the best of luck in your future endeavors," he said sincerely, his words echoing with a sense of promise and possibility.

As Arjun shook the HR executive's hand, he couldn't help but feel a surge of excitement coursing through him. The road ahead might be challenging, but he was ready to embrace it with open arms, knowing that he had the support of his new colleagues and the opportunity to make a real difference in the world of sales.

As Arjun came out of the hall and basked in the joy of his unexpected success, his phone rang with Diya's name flashing on the screen. His heart skipped a beat as he answered the call, a rush of emotions flooding through him.

"Hey, Diya! How are you?" Arjun greeted, trying to keep his voice steady despite the whirlwind of feelings inside him.

"Arjun! Oh my gosh, I heard the news! Congratulations!" Diya's voice bubbled with genuine happiness, her excitement contagious even through the phone.

"Thank you, Diya! It means a lot coming from you," Arjun replied, his voice tinged with warmth and gratitude.

"See! I told you you're going to make it sooner or later! I always knew you had it in you, Arjun. You're destined for great things," Diya said earnestly, her words like a balm to his soul.

Arjun hesitated momentarily, the weight of unspoken words hanging heavy in the air. "Diya, I... I just wanted to say thank you. For everything," he began, his voice trailing off as he struggled to find the right words.

Diya's tone softened, sensing the turmoil in Arjun's voice. "Arjun, you don't have to thank me. I'm just happy to see you succeed," she reassured him, her words infused with warmth and understanding.

Arjun took a deep breath, steeling himself for what he knew he had to say. "Diya, I've… I've always cared about you. More than you'll ever know," he confessed, his heart pounding in his chest.

There was a moment of silence on the other end of the line, the weight of Arjun's words hanging heavy in the air. "Arjun, I… I appreciate your honesty. But you know how I feel," Diya replied gently, her voice tinged with regret.

Arjun felt a lump form in his throat, the sting of rejection piercing his heart once again. "Yeah, I know," he said quietly, a hint of sadness coloring his words.

"But Arjun, that doesn't change how much I value our friendship. You mean the world to me," Diya said sincerely, her words offering a glimmer of solace amidst the pain.

Arjun swallowed hard, the bitter taste of disappointment still lingering on his tongue. "I know, Diya. And you mean a lot to me, too," he said softly, his voice tinged with resignation.

"You have to move on, Arjun! See, you have made it to such a fantastic company! Focus on your career now. Be successful and happy. Promise me you will become the best in what you do!"

"I promise!"

Arjun couldn't help but feel a sense of closure wash over him as they exchanged a few more pleasantries. Despite the lingering ache in his heart, he knew it was time to let go of his unrequited love and embrace the friendship that had always been there for him. And as he hung up the phone, a small smile tugged at the corners of his lips, knowing that no matter what the future held, he would always cherish the moments he shared with Diya.

Arjun hung up the phone. A bittersweet acceptance settled over him. Despite the ache of unrequited love still lingering in his heart, he couldn't deny the warmth of Diya's friendship and support. With a deep breath, he turned his gaze towards the future, determined to forge ahead with newfound clarity and purpose.

Arjun's mind drifted back to his own interview experience. It had been a whirlwind of intensity and pressure, every question probing deeper and deeper into his capabilities and character.

"Arjun, could you tell us about a time when you faced a major challenge and how you overcame it?" the interviewer had asked, their gaze piercing as they waited for his response.

Arjun had taken a deep breath, marshaling his thoughts before launching into a detailed recounting of a particularly challenging project he had undertaken during college. Despite the pressure of the moment, he had managed to articulate his experiences and insights with clarity and conviction, his words flowing effortlessly as he recounted the obstacles he had faced and the strategies he had employed to overcome them.

"Very impressive, Arjun. Now, let's talk about your leadership style. How do you motivate and inspire your team to achieve their goals?" another interviewer had inquired, their tone thoughtful as they leaned forward, awaiting his answer.

Arjun had drawn upon his experiences as a team leader in various extracurricular activities, detailing his strategies to foster collaboration, communication, and mutual respect among team members. With each example he provided, his confidence had grown, and his passion for leadership shone through in his words and demeanor.

Despite the grueling nature of the interview, Arjun couldn't help but feel a sense of exhilaration as he recalled the adrenaline-fueled rush of articulating his thoughts and ideas under scrutiny. The one and a half hours had flown by in a blur, each minute packed with intense concentration and unwavering focus.

When he finally emerged from the interview room, his friends looked concerned, their eyebrows raised in disbelief at the length of his absence. Then came Abhijit's jesting inquiry, his voice laced with mock concern and playful curiosity.

"Buddy, were you okay in there? Did they have you solving complex equations or something? We were starting to worry!" Abhijit had joked, his words punctuated by a playful chuckle.

Arjun had laughed along with them, the tension of the interview dissipating into a shared moment of camaraderie and relief. But now, as he reflected on the experience, he couldn't help but marvel at the depth of engagement and intellectual challenge that had characterized the interview process.

Despite the difficulty of the questions and the pressure of the moment, Arjun knew that he had risen to the occasion, drawing upon his skills and knowledge to present himself in the best possible light. As he looked towards the future, he felt a renewed sense of confidence and determination, ready to tackle whatever challenges lay ahead with the same resilience and tenacity that had seen him through the interview.

Reflecting on his recent success in securing a job, Arjun felt a glimmer of optimism. The world was full of endless possibilities, and he was determined to seize every opportunity that came his way. No longer bound by the weight of unfulfilled dreams, he was ready to embark on a new chapter of his life with renewed vigor and determination.

With a newfound sense of confidence, Arjun began to envision a future filled with exciting challenges and new adventures. He knew that obstacles would be encountered, but he was determined to face them head-on, armed with the lessons learned from his past experiences.

Arjun couldn't help but feel the excitement coursing through his veins as he took his first steps toward his future. The road ahead might be uncertain, but he was ready to embrace it with open arms, knowing that whatever lay ahead, he would face it with courage, resilience, and an unwavering belief in himself.

Arjun took a bold step into the unknown with a smile and a sense of anticipation in his heart, ready to write the next chapter of his story with courage, determination, and a newfound sense of purpose. Now he was no more a student of a college. Now, he would work for ZenCorp Insurance in Mumbai. He would be a Sales Manager. Or so it would seem!

2

City of Dreams!

As Arjun's train pulled into Mumbai, he peered out the window with wide eyes, expecting the city of dreams to welcome him with open arms. But what he found was a chaotic carnival of colors, chaos, and confusion.

Stepping onto the platform, Arjun felt like he had stumbled onto the set of a Bollywood blockbuster gone awry. The sights, the sounds, the smells—all hit him at once, like a slapstick comedy routine performed by a cast of thousands.

The platform was a riot of activity, with people rushing past in every direction like characters in a frenzied dance number. The air was thick with the scent of spices, sweat, and diesel fumes, a heady concoction that left Arjun feeling dizzy and disoriented.

Navigating through the crowd was like trying to swim against the tide in a tsunami of humanity. Everywhere he looked, there was a cacophony of noise and movement: honking horns, shouting vendors, and the incessant chatter of passersby. It was as if the entire city had turned into a live-action movie set, and Arjun was just an extra trying to find his mark.

Lost in the station's labyrinthine maze, Arjun felt like Alice tumbling down the rabbit hole into Wonderland. Signs in unfamiliar languages loomed overhead, and their meaning lost on him as he tried in vain to decipher their cryptic messages.

Desperate for guidance, Arjun approached a group of locals, his voice trembling as he asked for directions. But his attempts were met with blank stares and hurried brush-offs, leaving him feeling more lost than ever in this sea of strangers.

With each passing moment, Arjun's sense of disorientation deepened, his anxiety mounting with every step he took. He felt like a fish out of water, floundering in an ocean of chaos and confusion.

But amidst the madness, Arjun clung to a glimmer of hope. Deep down, he knew that he was capable of navigating this unfamiliar terrain, of finding his way through the maze of Mumbai's streets and alleys to his destination—the Headquarters of the Zencorp Insurance Company.

And so, with determination in his heart and a sense of humor that could rival any stand-up comedian's, Arjun squared his shoulders and plunged headlong into the bustling throng, ready to embrace the challenges and adventures that awaited him in the city of dreams. It would be one heck of a rollercoaster ride, and Arjun was ready to buckle up and enjoy the show.

After flagging down a taxi just outside the station, Arjun found himself at the headquarters in Dadar, Mumbai. Stepping into the third-floor office, he was greeted by a flurry of activity. The reception area was bustling with energy, adorned with traditional Indian artwork and plush seating that exuded an air of sophistication.

Approaching the receptionist with a polite "Hello," Arjun introduced himself, his excitement palpable as he caught his breath. "I'm here for my joining," he said with a smile, his voice tinged with anticipation.

The receptionist, a young woman, responded with an air of professionalism, her expression neutral. "Hello, can I see your appointment letter?" she asked politely, her tone suggesting she had dealt with countless new joiners before.

As Arjun eagerly presented his letter, his enthusiasm got the better of him, and he accidentally knocked over a small potted plant on the reception desk. Soil scattered across the counter, and Arjun's face flushed crimson with embarrassment as he fumbled to catch the falling plant.

The receptionist stifled a giggle behind her hand, her eyes twinkling with amusement. "Oops, looks like we have a bit of a green thumb here!" she teased, offering Arjun a knowing smile.

Mortified, Arjun mumbled an apology and hastily tried to clean up the mess, his cheeks burning with embarrassment. But the receptionist waved off his efforts with a laugh, her warm demeanor putting him at ease.

"No worries, Mr. Arjun. Accidents happen," she reassured him, her laughter infectious. "Now, please proceed to the conference room and be seated. Our HR manager will be with you shortly."

Grateful for her understanding, Arjun nodded sheepishly and made his way to the conference room, the memory of his clumsy introduction lingering like a comedic punchline in his mind. As he settled into his seat, he couldn't help but chuckle at the absurdity of it all. What a beginning to the first day of his first job! But after all, what's a new job without a little bit of chaos to keep things interesting?

The conference room was a hive of activity, with a mix of fresh-faced graduates and seasoned professionals filling the plush chairs around the table. The air buzzed with excitement and anticipation as Arjun took his seat among them, marveling at the diverse group of individuals gathered for their induction into the company. It was a scene that perfectly encapsulated the energy and vibrancy of Mumbai's corporate world, a melting pot of talent and ambition ready to tackle whatever challenges lay ahead.

As Arjun settled into his seat, he found himself in the middle of the room. To his left sat a young man with a guitar slung over his shoulder, a wide grin plastered across his face. His eyes sparkled with enthusiasm, and there was an infectious energy about him that seemed to light up the room.

"Hey there!" the young man chirped, extending a hand toward Arjun with a friendly smile. "I'm Rishi. Nice to meet you!"

Arjun returned the smile, feeling instantly at ease in Rishi's presence. "Hi, I'm Arjun. Likewise, nice to meet you too!"

Rishi nodded towards the guitar propped up against his chair. "I hope you don't mind the musical addition to our little gathering here," he joked, his tone lighthearted. I figured I'd bring a bit of cheer to the proceedings!"

Arjun chuckled, admiring Rishi's carefree attitude. "Not at all! It's great to see someone so upbeat on their first day. What made you bring the guitar?"

Rishi shrugged, a mischievous glint in his eye. "Oh, you know, just in case we need a bit of entertainment during the breaks."

"That's great! But it seems unlikely that you will get to play it at all in this corporate environment!"

Their conversation flowed easily, with Rishi regaling Arjun with stories of his college days and his excitement about starting his career. Despite their different backgrounds, they found common ground in their shared enthusiasm for the future.

"So, Arjun, what about you? Excited for your first day?" Rishi asked, leaning in with genuine interest.

Arjun nodded, a smile playing on his lips. "Definitely! Nervous, too, but mostly excited. It's a big step, you know?"

Rishi grinned, his enthusiasm infectious. "Oh, I hear you! But hey, we're in this together, right? Just think of it as the start of a new adventure!"

And as they continued to chat and laugh together, Arjun couldn't help but feel grateful for the chance encounter with Rishi. In a room full of strangers, he had found a friend, someone who made the daunting prospect of starting a new job seem a little less intimidating. And as they shared stories and jokes, Arjun did not know that this was just the beginning of a beautiful friendship.

As Arjun and Rishi continued their conversation, the atmosphere in the conference room shifted as the door swung open and a lady HR entered with a warm smile. She exuded confidence and authority, her presence commanding the attention of everyone in the room.

"Good morning, everyone! I'm Priya, your HR manager," she announced, her voice carrying a soothing tone. "Welcome to Zencorp Insurance. We're thrilled to have you all on board."

Arjun and Rishi exchanged a glance, both impressed by Priya's demeanor and professionalism. As she began to speak, they listened intently, eager to learn more about their new company.

"I won't bore you with a long speech," Priya continued, her smile widening. "But I do want to take a moment to tell you a bit about our company and what we stand for."

As Priya spoke, her words painted a picture of a company that valued integrity, innovation, and teamwork. She spoke passionately about the company's mission to provide the best possible service to its clients and the opportunities for growth and development available to employees.

"And now, onto some practical matters," Priya said, her tone becoming more business-like. "As you all know, finding accommodation in Mumbai can be quite challenging. So, we've arranged for hotel accommodations for each of you for the next fifteen days."

Arjun and Rishi exchanged a glance, relieved at the prospect of having a place to stay while they sorted out their living arrangements in the city.

"Tomorrow, you'll be reporting to your respective branches and meeting your reporting managers," Priya continued, her gaze sweeping over the room. "But for now, I encourage you to finish your paperwork here, settle into your hotel rooms, and start exploring the city. Mumbai has a lot to offer, and I want you to make the most of your time here."

As Priya finished speaking, Rishi couldn't help but be captivated by her poise and charm. Leaning over to Arjun, he whispered with a playful grin, "I think I'm in love with her. Maybe I should ask her for some personal guidance on finding accommodation."

Arjun chuckled, shaking his head at Rishi's antics. "I think you might want to focus on finding a place to stay first. Besides, there might be a possibility that she is either married or engaged already. Just check that ring on her finger,"

As they shared a laugh, Arjun couldn't help but feel grateful for Rishi's lighthearted humor, a welcome distraction from the nerves and excitement of their first day on the job. And as they prepared to embark on their new adventure in Mumbai, they knew that they could tackle anything that came their way with each other's support.

As Arjun and Rishi sat down to fill out their paperwork, they couldn't help but continue their conversation about Priya, the HR manager.

"Hey, do you think Priya is a universal name for HR managers in every company?" Arjun quipped, his tone playful as he scribbled away on his form.

Rishi chuckled, shaking his head in amusement. "I don't know, but if it is, they must all be as charming as our Priya."

Their attention then turned to another guy in the room who was filling out his paperwork at lightning speed, his pen practically a blur as he raced through the forms.

"Wow, look at that guy go," Arjun remarked, impressed by the efficiency of their fellow new joiner. "He's like a paperwork ninja!"

Rishi grinned, his eyes twinkling with mischief. "Yeah, I bet he's been practicing filling out forms since he was in diapers. Probably has a black belt in paperwork."

The two friends shared a laugh, their banter easing the tension of their first day on the job. And as they continued to joke and fill out their forms, they made a decision together.

"You know what, Arjun? We should stick together and look for a room in Mumbai together. We could be roommates," Rishi suggested, his tone earnest as he glanced at his friend.

Arjun nodded in agreement, grateful for Rishi's companionship. "Yeah, that sounds like a plan. Having a friend like you in this crazy city is a godsend."

But even as they made their plans, Rishi couldn't resist making one last joke about Priya, his grin turning mischievous.

"Hey, I wish Priya could join us in our room hunt," he teased, wagging his eyebrows suggestively. "I'm sure she'd love to help us find the perfect accommodation."

Arjun rolled his eyes, chuckling at his friend's antics. "Oh, Rishi. Stop it now! Don't you see that paperwork Ninja has already submitted his paperwork and left? And we still have heaps of forms to fill!"

"You are right. Let's fill them all quickly and submit them. Then we shall move to the hotel and look for a permanent accommodation."

And with that, the two friends continued their paperwork, their laughter echoing through the conference room as they looked forward to their adventures in Mumbai.

As Arjun and Rishi settled into the taxi on their way to the hotel, they couldn't help but continue their conversation about their past lives and ambitions.

"So, Arjun, tell me about yourself. What were you like before joining the corporate world?" Rishi asked, his curiosity evident in his voice.

Arjun glanced out the window momentarily, lost in thought, before replying, "Well, I just graduated from college. Spent most of my time buried in books and dreaming of making it big in the corporate world."

Rishi nodded, listening intently. "Ah, the classic college dream. I can relate. What about Mumbai? Have you heard anything about life here? And what about Ghatkopar where you have been assigned to?"

Arjun shrugged, a hint of uncertainty in his voice. "Not much, to be honest. Just the usual stories about the fast-paced lifestyle and the crazy traffic. Oh, and I've heard Ghatkopar is a bit… well, let's just say it's not the most glamorous place in Mumbai. What about you?"

Rishi laughed, the sound filling the taxi with warmth. "Guess what?"

With a mischievous grin, Rishi waved his joining letter in front of Arjun, excitement dancing in his eyes. "Dadar office, right from the Headquarters itself!"

Arjun's eyebrows shot up in surprise as he read the letter over Rishi's shoulder. "Dadar office? That's just opposite the headquarters on the same floor and down the hall from Priya's desk!"

Rishi chuckled, a twinkle of amusement in his eye. "Looks like I'll have a front-row seat to the Priya show every day!"

The two friends continued to joke and laugh as they made their way through the bustling streets of Mumbai. But as they neared their destination, Arjun couldn't shake the feeling of unease that had been gnawing at him since they had entered the office.

"You know, Rishi, I couldn't help but notice something strange back there," Arjun said, his voice tinged with uncertainty.

Rishi frowned, sensing his friend's unease. "What do you mean?"

"Well, it's just that… none of the employees in the office seemed happy," Arjun explained, furrowing his brow in thought. "I mean, they were all going about their work, but there was this… heaviness in the air. Like they were all just going through the motions."

Rishi fell silent, contemplating Arjun's observation. "Do you think it's something we should be worried about?" he asked, his voice tinged with concern.

Arjun shrugged, his mind swirling with questions. "I don't know, Rishi. But it got me thinking – is this what our lives are going to be like now? Is the cheerful, carefree life we had in college going to change drastically?"

The question hung in the air, unanswered. And as the taxi pulled up to their hotel, Arjun couldn't shake the feeling that their new life in Mumbai was going to be more challenging than they had ever imagined. But for now, all they could do was wait and see what the future held.

3

The Branch Office

As Arjun stepped into the Ghatkopar branch office of Zencorp Insurance, he was met with a scene straight out of a chaotic Bollywood movie. The atmosphere was electric with energy, but not the kind that inspired confidence. Instead, it crackled with tension and urgency, the air filled with the sounds of ringing phones, raised voices and hurried footsteps.

People rushed past him, barely sparing him a glance as they hurried about their tasks, their faces etched with stress and determination. Arjun couldn't help but feel a wave of apprehension washed over him as he navigated through the sea of desks and cubicles, trying to find his way to his branch manager's office.

Finally reaching the door marked "Sharat Kabra - Branch Manager," Arjun hesitated momentarily before knocking tentatively. The door swung open, revealing a middle-aged man seated behind a cluttered desk, his brow furrowed in concentration as he spoke into a phone.

Without looking up, the branch manager waved at Arjun impatiently, his tone brusque as he continued his conversation in rapid-fire Hindi. Arjun cleared his throat nervously, feeling like a dog caught in headlights as he stood before his new superior.

"Um, excuse me, sir? I'm Arjun, the new recruit," he ventured, his voice barely audible over the din of the office.

The branch manager finally glanced up, his expression one of mild annoyance as he took in Arjun's presence. "Ah, yes. The fresh recruit," he replied dismissively, his tone dripping with condescension. "Well, don't just stand there. Sit down and let's get started."

Feeling like a fish out of water, Arjun sank into the chair opposite the branch manager, his nerves jangling with uncertainty. But as the branch manager launched into a tirade about the job's expectations and demands, Arjun couldn't help but feel a sinking sensation in the pit of his stomach.

It was clear that his new boss had little patience for rookies like him, and the daunting reality of his new role began to sink in. As he listened to the branch manager's stern words and disparaging remarks, Arjun couldn't shake the feeling that he was way over his head. He watched as Sharat summoned a subordinate named Devraj into the room with a curt command. Devraj hesitated, clearly reluctant to comply, as he muttered something about having a lot of work to do. But the branch manager's stern insistence left him with no choice but to obey.

As Arjun followed Devraj into the bustling office area, he couldn't shake the sinking feeling in his stomach. Devraj motioned towards a row of empty chairs and tables, handing Arjun a list of names and phone numbers.

"Here, start making calls to schedule appointments with these people," Devraj instructed briskly, his tone leaving no room for argument.

Arjun hesitated, glancing down at the list with furrowed brows. "But I don't even know anything about the insurance products we're supposed to sell," he protested, a note of uncertainty creeping into his voice.

Devraj shrugged nonchalantly. "You'll pick it up as you go. Right now, just focus on setting up those appointments," he replied, his tone matter-of-fact.

Reluctantly, Arjun picked up the phone and dialed the first number on the list. After a few rings, someone answered, and Arjun launched into his pitch, stumbling over his words as he tried to explain the purpose of the call.

"Hello, this is Arjun calling from Zencorp Insurance. I'm calling to schedule an appointment to discuss our insurance products," he began tentatively.

But before he could finish his sentence, the voice on the other end interrupted him with a barrage of expletives, leaving Arjun stunned and speechless.

Devraj, who had been watching from nearby, couldn't help but smirk at Arjun's predicament. "Welcome to the world of insurance sales, kid," he remarked dryly, a hint of amusement in his voice.

Undeterred, Arjun continued to make calls, each one met with varying degrees of hostility and rejection. With each unsuccessful attempt, his frustration grew until finally, after what felt like an eternity, he hung up the phone in defeat.

"I couldn't schedule a single appointment," Arjun admitted, his voice tinged with frustration.

Devraj shrugged, unfazed by Arjun's lack of success. "Don't worry about it. It takes time to get the hang of things. Just keep at it," he replied, his tone oddly reassuring.

But as Arjun stared down at the list of names in front of him, the weight of his new responsibilities bearing down on him, he couldn't help but wonder if he was cut out for this ruthless world of insurance sales. As he prepared to make yet another call, the question lingered in his mind: would he ever find success in this cutthroat industry, or was he destined to be just another casualty of the corporate machine?

Arjun's phone buzzed, and he saw Rishi's name flashing on the screen. With a sigh of relief, he answered the call, eager to commiserate with his friend.

"Hey, Rishi, how's it going?" Arjun greeted, his voice heavy with exhaustion.

Rishi's voice came through the line, mirroring Arjun's weariness. "Oh, it Seems like I stepped into a hornet's nest today," he replied with a hint of resignation.

Arjun chuckled dryly. "Tell me about it. I've been getting an earful from my boss all day. And to top it off, I couldn't schedule a single appointment," he lamented.

Rishi let out a dramatic groan. "Well, at least you didn't have one, Mr. Gupta, yelling at you in three different languages. I'm pretty sure I'm fluent in profanity now," he quipped.

"Ah, that's the spirit! I'm already feeling a tad bit lighter! But doesn't today's experience starkly contrast with Priya's enchanting talk from yesterday?" remarked Arjun.

"Oh, if it weren't for catching glimpses of her in the office, I don't think I could have survived today's ordeal!" exclaimed Rishi.

Despite their frustrations, the two friends couldn't help but find humor in their misfortune. They exchanged stories of their disastrous first day on the job, laughing at the absurdity of it all.

But amidst the jokes and banter, Rishi's tone turned serious as he shared his latest development. "Hey, so I spoke to a property dealer, and he's going to show us a house for rent in Chembur. He says it's exactly the palace we are looking for. But the rent is sky-high, so we'll need another person to share it with us," he explained.

Arjun's interest was piqued at the mention of finding a place to stay. "Chembur, you said? I'm in. Let's go check it out," he replied eagerly.

And so, with a mix of laughter and determination, Arjun and Rishi made plans to embark on their next adventure together, navigating the trials and tribulations of Mumbai's cutthroat corporate world side by side, one joke at a time.

4
The Underwriter

Arjun and Rishi stood in front of the house, their jaws dropping at its seemingly minuscule size despite being advertised as having three rooms. They exchanged incredulous glances before turning to the property dealer, who wore a smug grin as if he had just revealed a hidden treasure.

Arjun scratched his head in disbelief. "Are you sure this is the right place? It looks more like a dollhouse than a living space."

The property dealer chuckled, his laughter echoing off the cramped walls. "Welcome to Mumbai, gentlemen! Space here is as rare as an honest politician. You've got to make do with what you've got!"

Rishi nodded, a wry smile playing on his lips. "I guess we'll have to become experts at playing Tetris with our furniture," he quipped, envisioning a comical game of stacking chairs and tables like puzzle pieces.

The property dealer nodded in agreement. "Exactly! And if you think finding this place was tough, just wait until you try to find a roommate to fill that extra room. Mumbai is a city of dreams, but finding affordable housing? That's the real nightmare!"

Arjun let out a resigned sigh. "Well, looks like we're stuck between a rock and a hard place. What do you think, Rishi? Shall we take the plunge and become the proud tenants of this shoebox?"

Rishi grinned, his eyes sparkling with mischief. "Why not? After all, what's a little claustrophobia among friends? Let's do it!"

And so, with laughter echoing through the narrow hallways of their potential new home, Arjun, Rishi, and the property dealer set off on the quirky quest to find the elusive third musketeer to complete their trio of roommates in the bustling metropolis of Mumbai.

As Arjun and Rishi made their way to the Dadar headquarters for the HR briefing, Rishi couldn't help but chatter excitedly about the possibility of seeing Priya again.

"Hey, Arjun, you think we'll get to see Priya today?" Rishi asked with a mischievous grin.

Arjun rolled his eyes, knowing full well where Rishi's thoughts were drifting. "Focus, Rishi. We're here for the briefing, not to ogle at Priya," he reminded his friend with a chuckle.

But as they entered the office, their attention was immediately drawn to the same guy they had seen on their first day, furiously working through stacks of papers with the efficiency of a seasoned pro.

"O look! The Paperwork Ninja!" Arjun exclaimed, nodding towards him.

"That guy seriously doesn't know the meaning of 'taking it easy'! He's like a human tornado, leaving a trail of paperwork in his wake," Rishi quipped, shaking his head in disbelief."

Their observations were interrupted as they were ushered into the conference room, where Priya stood at the front, looking as poised and elegant as ever in her pantsuit. Rishi couldn't tear his eyes away from her, his mind wandering to thoughts of their previous encounter.

As Priya began to brief them about the upcoming 15-day induction program in Jodhpur, Rishi found himself lost in admiration, his gaze lingering on her lovely face. And in a moment of boldness, he couldn't resist the urge to flirt with her. With a mischievous twinkle in his eye, Rishi leaned forward, directing a question at Priya about the induction program. "So, Priya, will there be any chance to ride camels in Jodhpur? I've always wanted to be a desert explorer!"

Priya's lips curved into a playful smile as she replied, "Well, Rishi, while camel riding isn't on the agenda, I can promise you plenty of other exciting activities that don't involve getting sand in your shoes."

Undeterred, Rishi continued with another question, "What about a midnight treasure hunt in the palace gardens? I've got a knack for finding hidden gems!"

Priya chuckled, her eyes dancing with amusement. "As intriguing as that sounds, Rishi, I'm afraid our program focuses more on professional development than nocturnal escapades. But who knows, maybe you'll uncover some hidden talents along the way!"

Arjun couldn't help but suppress a laugh at Rishi's attempts to charm Priya with his whimsical inquiries. It seemed his friend was determined to add a touch of adventure to even the most mundane of activities.

Arjun shot Rishi a stern look, silently urging him to rein in his flirtatious antics before they landed him in hot water. "Rishi, seriously, knock it off. This isn't college anymore. You could get fired for this kind of talk," he chided in a hushed tone.

"Can't help it, man! She is so amazing. She could be my soulmate!" Rishi exclaimed.

"At this point in time, we need a roommate. Focus on that," said Arjun.

Rishi rolled his eyes but relented under Arjun's earnest gaze. "Fine, fine, I'll behave. So how should we go about finding this elusive third roommate?"

Before Arjun could respond, they were interrupted by the arrival of the paper ninja himself, who had overheard their conversation about finding a third roommate.

"Hey, guys, my name is Saurabh. Sorry to eavesdrop, but I couldn't help but overhear you're looking for a roommate," He interjected, his eyes darting between Arjun and Rishi.

Arjun exchanged a surprised glance with Rishi, taken aback by Saurabh's sudden appearance. "Uh, yeah, we are. But how did you...?" he trailed off, his curiosity piqued.

Saurabh chuckled, his demeanor relaxed despite his ninja-like efficiency with paperwork. "Let's just say I have a knack for picking up on things. Plus, I've been on the hunt for an affordable room myself," he explained with a casual shrug.

Rishi's eyes lit up with excitement. "Well, what do you know? Looks like we've found our third musketeer!" he exclaimed, unable to contain his enthusiasm.

Arjun shot Rishi a grateful smile, relieved to have their housing dilemma resolved so unexpectedly. "Welcome aboard, Saurabh. Looks like this crazy adventure just got a whole lot crazier," he remarked with a chuckle. Then he glanced at Saurabh with a hint of uncertainty. "So, Saurabh, you'd be okay sharing a place with a couple of freshers like us?"

Saurabh raised an eyebrow, a mischievous twinkle in his eye. "What makes you think I'm some seasoned veteran?" he retorted with a smirk.

Arjun blinked in surprise. "Oh, uh, we just assumed... I mean, you seem so... organized?" he stammered, struggling to find the right words.

Saurabh chuckled, shaking his head. "Well, surprise! I'm a fresher, too. But don't worry, I've got skills," he declared confidently.

Rishi leaned in, curiosity piqued. "Skills, huh? What do you do here, Saurabh?"

Saurabh grinned, puffing out his chest proudly. "I'm an underwriter."

Arjun and Rishi exchanged puzzled glances. "Under... what now?" Arjun asked, scratching his head in confusion.

Saurabh laughed, realizing their confusion. "An underwriter evaluates and assesses risks for insurance companies. Think of me as the gatekeeper who decides whether or not to approve insurance policies that you sell," he explained.

Rishi's eyes widened in mock horror. "Ah, so you're like an undertaker, but for insurance policies!" he exclaimed, unable to resist the comparison.

The trio laughed at Rishi's comparison, their bond strengthening with each shared chuckle. As they continued to chat and joke, it became clear that despite their differences, they were already forming a strong friendship bound by humor and camaraderie.

5
The Induction

As the sun dipped low on the horizon, Arjun, Rishi, and Saurabh found themselves happily settled into their new rented house, reveling in the excitement of their upcoming journey to Jodhpur for fifteen days of induction away from their dreaded bosses.

While Arjun and Rishi concocted elaborate schemes to flunk the office day under the guise of a field visit, Saurabh, being the diligent underwriter that he was, resigned himself to a day of desk-bound drudgery. He would be joining them directly at the railway station in the evening.

With a backpack slung over his shoulders and a mischievous grin plastered on his face, Rishi sauntered into the office, ready to put his flunking plan into action. He wanted to mark his attendance on the biometric device and slip out of the office. But as soon as he was trying to do so, his boss called upon him unexpectedly.

As Rishi's boss beckoned him over to his desk, a sinking feeling settled in the pit of Rishi's stomach. "Just my luck," he muttered under his breath, already anticipating the impending disaster.

"Yes, Boss!"

"Before you head out, shoot an email to all the insurance agents, instructing them to report directly to me in your absence."

"Got it, Boss!"

With trembling hands, Rishi reached into his bag to retrieve his laptop, only to be met with chaos as his charger decided to play hide-and-seek at the bottom of his bag. Frantically trying to conceal his packed backpack from the prying eyes of his boss, one of his underwear suddenly popped out of his backpack as if trying to make a daring escape.

In a panic, Rishi scrambled to conceal the unexpected intruder, praying that no one had witnessed the unexpected wardrobe malfunction. Thankfully, his embarrassment remained confined to his own mortified blushes as he hastily composed the required email and made an exit from the office.

Outside, Arjun was waiting, his eyes twinkling with mischief as Rishi regaled him with the tale of his underwear's ill-timed appearance. With laughter ringing in their ears, the duo set off for a day of sun, sand, and endless mischief at Juhu Beach.

As they lounged in the warm embrace of the sand, Arjun couldn't resist teasing Rishi about the potential consequences of his rogue underwear encounter. "Just imagine if Priya had been the unfortunate victim of your airborne undergarment! What if she was there and your underwear fell upon her head?" he exclaimed, doubling over with laughter at the absurdity of the thought.

With their worries washed away by the gentle lapping of the waves, Arjun and Rishi reveled in the simple joy of friendship and the promise of adventures yet to come as they boarded the train to Jodhpur. Ready to embark on their next escapade with hearts full of laughter and anticipation, Saurabh had also joined them at the station.

As the sun dipped below the horizon, casting a golden hue over the bustling city of Jodhpur, Arjun, Rishi, and Saurabh found themselves at the gates of the prestigious university where their induction program was set to take place. Excitement bubbled within them as they joined the throngs of fresh-faced recruits from across the country, all eager to embark on their journey into the world of insurance.

As they settled into the bustling atmosphere of the university, Rishi couldn't contain his excitement. "Hey, Arjun, Saurabh, check out the energy here! It's like a mini India in one place!"

Arjun chuckled, nodding in agreement. "Yeah, it's pretty amazing to see so many different people coming together for the same purpose. Who knew insurance could bring us all together like this?"

Saurabh chimed in with a wry grin. "Well, they say insurance is all about managing risks. Looks like they're starting with the risk of putting us all in one room!"

Their laughter echoed through the halls as they made their way to the cultural programs, where Rishi wasted no time in joining the musical festivities. "Alright, folks, get ready for a musical treat! I'm about to show you all why they call me the king of good times!"

Amidst the spirited singing and friendly competition, Arjun couldn't help but feel a sense of camaraderie growing among the recruits. "You know, guys, as crazy as this all is, there's something special about being part of this journey together. Here's to new beginnings!"

Saurabh raised an eyebrow with a smirk. "Ah, spoken like a true insurance salesman. Always finding the silver lining, even in a sea of policies and premiums!"

Their banter continued into the training sessions, where Saurabh's dry humor provided a welcome respite from the dense material. "Alright, folks, brace yourselves for another riveting discussion on actuarial tables and risk assessment. Try to contain your excitement!"

Arjun and Rishi chuckled, grateful for Saurabh's ability to inject some levity into the proceedings. "Hey, Saurabh, if anyone can make insurance sound interesting, it's you!" Rishi quipped, earning a playful shove from his friend.

As the days passed and the initial excitement of the induction program began to fade, Arjun found himself grappling with a sense of loneliness that crept in when the laughter died down, and the lights dimmed. Surrounded by the jovial camaraderie of his fellow recruits and the familiar sights of the university campus, memories of his college days flooded back, each one tinged with bittersweet nostalgia.

In the quiet moments of solitude, Arjun couldn't help but find his thoughts drifting to Diya, the girl who had once captured his heart with her laughter and kindness. With a heavy heart, he reminisced about the sweet moments they had shared, the late-night conversations and stolen glances that had filled his college days with warmth and joy.

But as he reached for his phone, fingers trembling with uncertainty, doubt gnawed at him. Would reaching out to Diya only reopen old wounds? Would she even want to hear from him after all this time?

Despite his misgivings, Arjun couldn't shake the feeling of longing that lingered within him. With a deep breath, he mustered the courage to send her a message, pouring his heart out in a few simple words that echoed with the echoes of a past love.

Hours passed, each minute feeling like an eternity as Arjun waited with bated breath for a response that never came. The silence weighed heavily on him, a tangible reminder of the gulf that had formed between him and the girl he had once held so dear.

In the stillness of the night, Arjun grappled with a tumult of emotions, wondering if he had made a mistake in reaching out or if, perhaps, in the end, some memories were meant to remain just that – memories.

As they absorbed the wealth of knowledge being imparted to them, Arjun, Rishi, and Saurabh found themselves forming bonds with their fellow recruits, united by a shared sense of purpose and a healthy dose of humor. And as they looked ahead to the challenges and opportunities awaiting them in the insurance industry, they knew they were ready to take on whatever came their way, armed with knowledge, friendship, and a healthy dose of laughter.

Or so they thought!

6
The Toil Begins

Arjun's heart sank as he entered his office, greeted by the stern gaze of Sharat, who wasted no time in cutting straight to the chase.

"Alright, Arjun, glad to see you back. Now that you've had your little induction vacation, it's time to get down to business. The honeymoon period is over," Sharat declared, his voice dripping with disdain.

Arjun braced himself for what was to come, steeling his nerves as Sharat continued with a ruthless efficiency that bordered on abuse.

"You've got a target of 25 lakhs, Arjun. And let me make one thing clear: this isn't some Hollywood movie where a wise old sage guides you through the intricacies of the trade. Here at Zencorp, we believe in tough love. We'll tie your hands and toss you into the deep end, expecting you to swim. You may have learned the theory of insurance, but selling it is a whole different ball game," Sharat barked, his words landing like a series of blows.

Arjun's jaw tightened as he struggled to maintain his composure in the face of Sharat's harsh words. He felt a surge of frustration welling up inside him, the weight of expectations pressing down on his shoulders like a leaden burden. As Arjun listened to Sharat's tirade, his gaze drifted past the glass door of the cabin to where Devraj stood, a sly grin playing on his lips as he made a throat-slitting gesture. Arjun's heart sank at the ominous warning, but he forced himself to maintain a neutral expression as he turned back to face Sharat.

"Understood, sir," Arjun replied evenly, his voice betraying none of the unease churning within him. "Where would you like me to sit?"

Sharat's response was as curt as ever, a sharp bark of, "There's no seating plan here, Arjun. Sales Managers are meant to be out in the field, not lounging around in the office. If you want a seat, you'll have to find one yourself."

With a resigned nod, Arjun stepped outside the cabin, scanning the sparse office for any available seating. To his dismay, there were hardly any chairs to be found, leaving him with few options.

It was then that Devraj, ever the opportunist, motioned for Arjun to join him on a stool nearby. "Come on, mate. Take a load off," he offered with a friendly smile.

Grateful for the gesture, Arjun nodded his thanks and settled onto the stool beside Devraj, grateful for the small semblance of camaraderie amidst the chaos of his new workplace. As he perched on the makeshift seat, Arjun couldn't help but wonder just what he had gotten himself into.

As he settled onto the stool beside Devraj, he couldn't help but feel a wave of frustration washing over him. "So, Devraj, how am I supposed to hit this target if I can't even sell insurance directly?" he asked, his voice tinged with exasperation.

Devraj leaned back in his chair, a knowing twinkle in his eye. "Ah, my dear Arjun, welcome to the wonderful world of insurance sales! You see, the key to success here is not through selling directly to customers but through our trusty insurance agents."

Arjun furrowed his brow in confusion. "But aren't they the ones who need a license from IRDA? And doesn't that take months?"

Devraj nodded sagely, tapping his chin thoughtfully. "Indeed, indeed. You have learnt a lot from your induction. But here's the kicker – our company has a little workaround for that pesky licensing process. We enroll them as service providers instead and offer them higher commissions. It's a win-win situation!"

Arjun's eyes widened in realization. "So, you're telling me we're bending the rules to make a profit?"

Devraj grinned mischievously. "You catch on faster than I thought, Arjun! Welcome to the world of corporate loopholes and shady dealings. Now, all you need to do is find some new service providers and watch those commissions roll in!"

The absurdity of the situation struck Arjun, and he couldn't help but laugh at the audacity of it all. "Well, I guess if you can't beat 'em, join 'em, right?"

Devraj clapped him on the back with a hearty chuckle. "That's the spirit, my friend! Embrace the chaos and let the commissions flow!"

Devraj slid a hefty stack of papers across the desk towards Arjun, a wry grin playing on his lips. "Here you go, Arjun. Your ticket to commission paradise."

Arjun glanced down at the list in front of him, eyes widening at the sheer volume of names scrawled across the page. "Wow, that's quite a roster. Who are these people?"

Devraj leaned in conspiratorially, his voice dropping to a hushed whisper. "These, my friend, are the unsung heroes of the insurance world – the ones who failed their IRDA exams or are knee-deep in the finance industry. Stockbrokers, credit card salesmen, or just some local uncle wanting to do some dhandha! They're hungry for a chance to make some real money."

"What does 'dhandha' mean?"

"Precisely what it sounds like! In the Mumbaiyya dialect, we don't say 'business', we say 'dhandha'!"

"Right!"

"And yes! Beware of the local uncles! They are the most shrewd business minds ever. They are hard negotiators. They will take everything from you but will give nothing back!"

Arjun's mind raced as he scanned the list, the gears turning as he processed the implications. "So, what's my role in all of this?"

Devraj grinned, tapping the papers with a flourish. "Your mission, should you choose to accept it, is to call each of these fine folks, set up meetings, and convince them to sign on as service providers for Zencorp. It's all about negotiation, my friend. You'll have to sweet-talk them, promise them the moon and stars if need be."

Arjun nodded slowly, the weight of the task ahead settling over him like a heavy blanket. "But what about commissions? I thought there were limits."

Devraj chuckled, shaking his head knowingly. "Ah, but that's where the beauty of being a service provider comes in. While IRDA guidelines may limit the commissions, as service providers, we have a little more leeway. It's all about playing the game Arjun. And with your charm and persuasion skills, I have no doubt you'll have them eating out of the palm of your hand in no time."

As Arjun took in Devraj's words, a sense of determination surged within him. Armed with his newfound knowledge and a list of potential recruits, he began frantically calling them one by one. Also he was happy that he had finally found someone like Devraj to guide him.

As Arjun dialed the numbers from the list, he braced himself for a rollercoaster ride of conversations. The first call connected, but to his dismay, he was greeted by the unmistakable sound of a disconnected line. Chuckling to himself, Arjun moved on to the next number.

"Hello, am I speaking to Mr. Sharma?" Arjun inquired politely.

A gruff voice on the other end responded with a string of colorful expletives, leaving Arjun scrambling to end the call before his ears were assaulted further.

Undeterred, Arjun pressed on, only to encounter a barrage of queries from the recipient on the other end. "What's the catch? How much will I make? Are there any hidden fees?" Arjun did his best to field the questions, but the relentless interrogation left him feeling like he was being cross-examined in a courtroom.

Just when he thought he had encountered every possible scenario, Arjun found himself on the line with a particularly shrewd negotiator. "Listen, kid, I'm not signing anything until I get a guarantee of at least a 20% commission," the voice insisted, leaving Arjun scrambling to keep up with the fast-paced bargaining.

But amid the chaos and confusion, there were moments of unexpected humor. A particularly cheeky respondent insisted on speaking in rhymes, while another claimed to be a long-lost relative of a Bollywood superstar, regaling Arjun with tales of their supposed family connections.

Through it all, Arjun couldn't help but laugh at the absurdity of it all. Each call brought with it a new challenge, a new opportunity for humor, and a lot of frustration.

As he continued to scroll through his list of potential leads, a sense of frustration began to gnaw at him. Despite his best efforts, not a single prospect seemed interested in what he had to offer. With each unanswered call, his anxiety mounted, exacerbated by the disapproving glances of Sharat as he made his rounds.

But just when Arjun was about to throw in the towel, a ray of hope appeared. As the phone rang on the other end, Arjun held his breath, hoping for a positive response. To his delight, Mr. Hiten picked up. He sounded quite pleasant.

"Is this Mr. Hiten?"

"Yes, speaking. How can I assist you?"

"Hello, Sir. This is Arjun calling from Zencorp Insurance Company. I have a fantastic opportunity for you where you can earn top-notch commissions by selling our insurance products!"

"Alright, sounds interesting."

"If you're interested, I can come over to your place and explain everything in detail. It'll only take half an hour of your time, but I guarantee it'll be worth it."

After a moment's consideration, Mr. Hiten agreed. "Alright, can you come and meet me at my home in Tilak Nagar at 4 in the evening?"

"Absolutely, sir! I'll be there!"

Ecstatic, Arjun practically bounced over to Devraj's desk to share the good news. "Devraj, you won't believe it! I finally got my first lead! Mr. Hiten has agreed to meet with me this afternoon!"

Devraj grinned, clapping Arjun on the back in congratulation. "That's fantastic news, Arjun! Now, let me give you some pointers on how to seal the deal."

As Devraj rattled off a list of tips and tricks, Arjun listened intently, his mind racing with anticipation. He thanked Devraj for his guidance before hurriedly gathering his things and heading out the door.

On the way to his meeting with Mr. Hiten, Arjun couldn't help but rehearse his pitch over and over again, mumbling to himself as he navigated the bustling streets of Mumbai. With each step, his excitement grew, fueled by the prospect of finally securing his first successful lead.

Arjun arrived at the designated meeting spot, his nerves tingling with anticipation. He stepped out of the taxi, his eyes widening in surprise as he took in his surroundings. The address he had been given had led him to a narrow alleyway in a dingy, slum-like area. It was a stark contrast to the sleek, modern office spaces he had grown accustomed to.

The alley was lined with crumbling buildings, their walls marred by graffiti and peeling paint. The narrow path was cluttered with debris and stray animals, adding to the sense of disarray. A group of children played nearby, their laughter echoing through the alley, a stark contrast to the otherwise grim environment.

As he navigated through the winding lanes, he noticed the makeshift stalls selling everything from vegetables to electronic goods. The air was thick with the smell of street food, mingling with the less pleasant odors of the area. He could hear the distant hum of traffic, but it felt worlds away from the buzzing, chaotic scene in front of him.

Finally, he arrived at the designated building. It was a dilapidated structure, with a narrow, rusted staircase leading up to the second floor. Taking a deep breath, he climbed the steps, the creaking sound under his feet adding to his apprehension. He knocked on the weathered wooden door, wondering what lay ahead in this unexpected setting.

Spotting Mr. Hiten waiting for him, he approached with a confident smile.

"Mr. Hiten, thank you so much for meeting with me today. I'm Arjun from Zencorp Insurance," he greeted warmly, extending his hand.

Mr. Hiten returned the handshake with a firm grip, a hint of curiosity in his eyes. "Pleasure to meet you, Arjun. You can start now."

With a practiced charm, Arjun launched into his pitch, outlining the benefits of becoming a service provider for Zencorp Insurance. He painted a vivid picture of the potential earnings and flexible working hours, all the while gauging Mr. Hiten's reactions for signs of interest.

As he spoke, Mr. Hiten listened attentively, nodding along thoughtfully. "It sounds like an intriguing opportunity. Now, wait for a moment."

Mr. Hiten gestured towards Arjun with a warm smile. "Mumbai's weather can be quite unforgiving, especially in this humidity. Let me fetch you a refreshing drink."

As Arjun settled into the chair, Mr. Hiten disappeared into the kitchen, returning moments later with a glass of Rooh Afzah sharbat. "Here you go, my friend. This will help quench your thirst."

"Thank you, sir," Arjun replied gratefully, taking a sip of the sweet beverage. "That's very kind of you."

Mr. Hiten then motioned toward the air conditioner and switched it on. "And let's not forget about the AC. We can't have you sweating buckets while we chat, now can we?"

Arjun chuckled appreciatively, feeling a wave of relief wash over him as the cool air enveloped him. "You're absolutely right, sir. Thank you for your hospitality."

With the pleasantries out of the way, Mr. Hiten moved towards a desk in his living room and retrieved a file. Arjun's eyes lit up with anticipation, assuming it was time to discuss the agreement.

But to his surprise, Mr. Hiten had other plans. "Now, Arjun, I've been listening to your pitch very carefully. Now, I'd like you to hear me out as well."

Curious, Arjun leaned in, eager to hear what Mr. Hiten had to say. However, instead of discussing the agreement, Mr. Hiten opened his file and began extolling the virtues of his own ULIP plan from another company.

With each persuasive argument and compelling statistic, Arjun found himself slowly but surely succumbing to Mr. Hiten's sales pitch. Before he knew it, he had agreed to purchase the ULIP plan, much to his own disbelief.

As he bid farewell to Mr. Hiten, Arjun couldn't help but feel like a fool for falling for his own sales tactics. With a wry grin, Mr. Hiten reassured him, "I'll definitely consider your offer, Arjun. But for now, let's just say you've bought into mine."

7

Crests and Troughs

Devraj doubled over with laughter, clutching his stomach as he gasped for breath. "Arjun, you're a legend! I can't believe you actually bought someone else's insurance plan! You've achieved negative targets, my friend!"

Arjun's cheeks burned with embarrassment. He was sitting on his chair, feeling like a deflated balloon.

Devraj's laughter was abruptly cut short when Sharat stormed into the room, his face contorted with rage. "What is going on here? Arjun, I hear you've been buying insurance instead of selling it. Have you lost your mind?"

Arjun cringed, feeling like a scolded child as Sharat berated him for his foolishness. "I'm sorry, sir. It was a mistake. I got carried away," he stammered, desperately trying to salvage some dignity.

But Sharat was having none of it. "You're a salesman, Arjun, not a client! I don't want to see you wasting time and money on personal purchases. Get back to work and start making some real sales!"

Defeated, Arjun slunk back to his desk and resumed his relentless cycle of phone calls and rejections. Day after day, he endured the crushing weight of failure, his confidence dwindling with each passing hour. He wasn't making any progress at all!

Arjun's heart sank as, after one week of zero progress, Sharat delivered the dreaded news. "Arjun, since you haven't made any progress with phone calls, I'm afraid we'll have to resort to more traditional methods. I want you to start selling door to door."

Arjun's face fell, his disappointment palpable. "Door to door?" he repeated incredulously. "But sir, is this the job of a Sales Manager?"

Sharat shook his head sternly. "Be a SalesMan first. Then think about being a Sales Manager! You young recruits want to be managers straight away, without any hard work. Get your hands dirty first. No excuses! This is your job, and you need to do whatever it takes to get results. Your target of twenty five lakhs still stands!"

Resigned to his fate, Arjun accepted the task and was handed a list of housing societies in the Ghatkopar area. Armed with brochures and a forced smile, he set out on foot, his shoes already pinching his blistered feet.

Arjun trudged along the bustling streets of Ghatkopar, the weight of his clipboard dragging him down like an anchor. Sharat's latest directive echoed in his mind, filling him with a sense of dread. Door-to-door sales? Seriously?

With a heavy sigh, Arjun glanced down at the list of housing societies clutched tightly in his hand. Each name seemed to mock him, a reminder of the daunting task ahead.

As he approached the first society on the list, Arjun couldn't help but feel a wave of apprehension washed over him. How was he supposed to convince complete strangers to buy home insurance when he could barely muster the enthusiasm himself?

Summoning whatever semblance of confidence he could muster, Arjun squared his shoulders and rang the doorbell of the nearest apartment. After what felt like an eternity, the door creaked open to reveal a skeptical-looking homeowner peering back at him.

"Good afternoon, sir! My name is Arjun, and I'm from Zencorp Insurance. I'm here to offer you a fantastic opportunity to protect your home and family with our comprehensive home insurance coverage," Arjun began, launching into his well-rehearsed spiel.

But before he could even finish his sentence, the homeowner cut him off with a dismissive wave of his hand. "Sorry, not interested," he muttered, already beginning to close the door.

Undeterred, Arjun scrambled to regain his footing. "Wait, sir! Please, just hear me out for a moment. You never know when disaster might strike, and with our insurance policy, you can have peace of mind knowing that your home is protected against any unforeseen circumstances," he pleaded, desperation creeping into his voice.

But it was no use. With a final click, the door slammed shut in Arjun's face, leaving him feeling dejected and defeated.

With each subsequent door he knocked on, Arjun's spirits sank lower and lower. Rejection after rejection wore him down, his feet throbbing with each painful step.

As the sun began to dip below the horizon, Arjun realized with a sinking heart that he had barely made a dent in his list of housing societies. Exhausted and demoralized, he trudged back to the office, his dreams of success crumbling around him with each blistered footfall.

The weekend evening breeze provided some respite from the scorching heat of the day as Arjun, Rishi, and Saurabh gathered on their terrace, seeking solace in each other's company. Arjun began to regale his friends with the tale of his exhausting day. His voice tinged with frustration.

"You wouldn't believe the day I've had," Arjun lamented, slumping down onto the floor. "I walked miles, knocking on door after door, only to be met with slammed doors and disinterested faces. No one wants to buy Zencorp's home Insurance Policy!"

Rishi nodded sympathetically, his own woes weighing heavily on his mind. "Tell me about it," he sighed. "I get yelled at by not only my immediate boss. By virtue of being in the headquarters, I am yelled at by the Regional Manager and the National Head too!"

"I am now convinced that we have been made complete fools by this company. They hired us as Sales Managers. But they are making us work like a Salesman! And my parents think I am some corporate bigshot! I feel so ashamed of myself. It's like I'm cursed with eternal gloom."

Saurabh listened intently, his brow furrowing in concern.

"You are so lucky Saurabh!" Arjun said gloomily, gesturing towards him. "You're always holed up in the cozy air-conditioned office, buried under piles of paperwork. Must be a breeze compared to our struggles."

Saurabh shook his head solemnly, his expression grave. "Oh, if only you knew," he replied, his voice tinged with sarcasm. "Approving and rejecting insurance policies may sound simple, but let me tell you, it's a jungle out there."

Arjun and Rishi exchanged puzzled glances, unable to comprehend Saurabh's plight. "What do you mean?" Arjun asked, curiosity piqued.

Saurabh leaned forward, his eyes gleaming with mischief. "You see, while you two are out battling the elements, I'm waging a war of paperwork," he explained. "Every policy proposal is like a minefield, waiting to explode with hidden clauses and fine print."

Rishi chuckled, unable to suppress a grin. "So you're saying your desk is a battlefield, and you're the valiant soldier fighting off the onslaught of paperwork?"

Saurabh nodded knowingly, a wry smile dancing on his lips. "You wouldn't believe the pressure I face with every case I handle," he admitted. "The sales team is constantly breathing down my neck, pushing me to prioritize their applications. And if that's not enough, the seniors themselves often pressure me to overlook incomplete applications. I'm damned if I do, doomed if I don't. You may not see my scars, but trust me, they're there."

Their eyes met, sharing a silent understanding of each other's struggles. As laughter filled the air, the trio found solace in their shared ordeals, their bonds strengthening amidst the challenges they faced.

"We're all sailing in the same boat, and that boat's name is Zencorp," Arjun quipped, his tone tinged with sarcasm.

Rishi, ever the optimist, proposed a change of scenery. "It's Saturday evening, guys. Let's ditch the cooking and head out for some drinks and dinner. What do you say?"

Saurabh grinned, his spirits lifted by the prospect. "Why the hell not? Let's do it!"

As the trio ventured out into the evening, determined to drown their sorrows in drinks and good food, they found themselves strolling down a dimly lit street, the LED lights of a nearby restaurant catching their attention. With its inviting glow and promise of respite from their troubles, they eagerly made their way towards it, unaware of the surprises that awaited them.

Entering the establishment, they were greeted by a haze of smoke and the unmistakable aroma of alcohol permeating the air. The dim lighting and pulsating music set the scene for an evening of revelry, or so they thought.

As Arjun, Rishi, and Saurabh stepped into the dimly lit establishment, Arjun couldn't help but remark, "This place looks... interesting."

Rishi chuckled nervously. "Yeah, it's got character, I'll give it that."

Taking a seat amidst the dimly lit ambiance, they placed their orders, anticipation mingling with the nervous energy that filled the room. It wasn't until the dim light revealed their surroundings that their expressions turned from excitement to bewilderment.

They found a table and settled in, but their uneasy laughter quickly turned to wide-eyed shock as the dim lighting revealed the scantily clad feminine figures surrounding them.

Saurabh's eyes widened in disbelief. "What in the world..."

Rishi tried to make sense of the situation. "Well, this wasn't exactly what I had in mind for a relaxing evening."

Before they could decide, a waitress approached, her outfit leaving little to the imagination. "What'll it be, boys?" she purred, her tone dripping with suggestive undertones.

Saurabh stammered, "Uh, just some water, please."

Rishi nodded in agreement, his voice strained. "Yeah, water sounds good."

As the waitress walked away, they exchanged incredulous glances. "What did we just walk into?" Arjun muttered, his disbelief palpable.

Their discomfort grew as they waited for their drinks. The other patrons' raucous laughter and clinking glasses provided an unsettling backdrop to their uneasy conversation.

Finally, their drinks arrived, and Rishi couldn't resist a quip. "Well, this certainly wasn't the type of bar we were looking for."

Arjun glanced around nervously. "Should we… maybe leave?"

"Yes, as quickly and quietly as possible!" said Saurabh.

As they made a dash for the exit, the bouncer erupted into a flurry of Marathi, "Are you not man enough," their words lost on the bewildered trio. Stepping out into the cool night air, they breathed a collective sigh of relief, their misadventure at the shady bar quickly becoming the stuff of legend among friends, with a shared nod of agreement. The bouncer's indignant shouts faded into the distance as they emerged back onto the street, their misadventure leaving them with a tale to tell for years to come.

"Dude! From Sales Manager to Sales Man. And now, not even Man enough!" quipped Arjun!

"Man, that property dealer made a fool out of us. The house that he got us is in a shady area!" screamed Rishi.

8
Breakthrough

"Hey, Devraj, you won't believe it! The president of one of the housing societies offered me to set up a stall there and sell insurance products!"

"Wow, that's fantastic news, Arjun! You should definitely go for it."

"They want us to set it up this Sunday. Would you be willing to come with me? Your expertise would be invaluable."

"Of course, Arjun! I'd be happy to help. Just let me know what arrangements need to be made, and I'll assist you every step of the way."

"Great! I'll handle the logistics, and you can help me with the paperwork and answer any technical questions the residents might have."

"Sounds like a plan! Let's make sure we have all the necessary brochures and documents ready to go. This could be a big opportunity for you.."

"Absolutely! Thanks for your support, Devraj. Together, I'm sure we can make this stall a huge success."

"No problem at all, Arjun. We're a team, and I'll always have your back. Let's make it happen!"

The day arrived. Arjun reached with the canopy kit and a bunch of brochures and pamphlets at the housing society. He unloaded all the stuff by himself and put it in the courtyard of the society. Devraj was nowhere to be seen. He called him.

"Hey Devraj, where are you? I'm at the housing society, and I need help in setting up the stall."

Devraj's groggy voice clearly showed he had just woken up, "Oh, hey, Arjun. Sorry, I'm not going to be able to make it today. Sunday is my only day off, and I really need to do my laundry."

"But Devraj, you yourself agreed to assist. I could really use your support here."

"I understand, Arjun, but I've already made plans for today. You'll be fine on your own. Just remember what we discussed and handle it like a pro."

"Alright, I guess I'll have to manage on my own. Thanks anyway, Devraj."

As Arjun sat behind the stall, the initial excitement of the morning had dwindled into a sense of dejection. Despite his efforts to set up the stall neatly and attractively, no one seemed to be approaching him. The morning sun cast long shadows across the quiet street, adding to his despondency. It felt as though his Sunday was slipping away, wasted on a futile endeavor.

With each passing moment, Arjun's thoughts grew more pessimistic. He couldn't shake the feeling of disappointment, not only in himself but also in the situation at hand. What would Sharat think of him now? Would he be seen as incapable or incompetent? These questions loomed over him, adding to his sense of defeat.

As he sat there, alone with his thoughts, Arjun couldn't help but wonder where things had gone wrong. Had he missed something crucial in his preparations? Was there something he could have done differently? These questions gnawed at him, amplifying his feelings of inadequacy.

Despite his best efforts to stay positive, Arjun couldn't shake the feeling of disappointment that hung heavy in the air. He could only hope that things would turn around soon, salvaging what was left of his Sunday and restoring some semblance of confidence in himself.

As the clock struck 11 AM, Arjun's fortunes took a turn for the better as a stream of curious residents began to gather around his stall. Excited chatter filled the air as they inquired about various insurance policies. Arjun, beaming with enthusiasm, eagerly explained the details, answering their questions with confidence.

Resident: "So, how does this health insurance work?"

Arjun: "Well, let me break it down for you. With our health insurance plan, you'll have access to a network of top hospitals and medical facilities, ensuring your peace of mind in times of need."

Another Resident: "And what about car insurance? I've been looking for a good deal."

Arjun: "You're in luck! Our car insurance policy offers comprehensive coverage at competitive rates. Plus, you'll enjoy hassle-free claim processing and quick resolution."

As the crowd swelled, Arjun found himself fielding inquiries about home insurance, life insurance, and more. With each successful explanation, his confidence soared, and soon, he was sealing deals left and right.

Arjun: "Congratulations! You're now covered with Zencorp's home insurance policy. Rest assured, your home is in safe hands."

The residents, pleased with Arjun's professionalism and the attractive policy offers, eagerly signed up, one after the other. Arjun's joy knew no bounds as he made his first sale and then another, each one more rewarding than the last.

At the end of each working day, it was a routine practice for Sharat to send a brief message to all the Sales Managers, whether he was present or not, consisting of just three alphabets followed by a question mark - "MTD?". This shorthand stood for Month Till Date, prompting each Sales Manager to reply with the business done for the month up to that particular day. For the past two months, Arjun had been sending nothing but a dismal "0" in response. This typically resulted in a barrage of abusive calls and threats of termination from Sharat. However, today marked a significant departure from the norm as Arjun proudly submitted an actual figure for the MTD. Within moments, a response arrived, surprising Arjun with its encouraging tone - "Well done! Expecting more."

The next day, Arjun strode into the office with a newfound sense of pride, his chest puffed out as he deposited a stack of insurance policy applications onto the desk beside Devraj's. Impressed by Arjun's accomplishment, he showered him with praise, commending his salesmanship and determination. However, Arjun's joy was short-lived as he realized he needed assistance to process the policies.

"Devraj, how do I go about getting these policies processed?"

"Ah, that's a crucial step indeed. You'll need an agent code to register these policies, but don't worry, I've got you covered."

Arjun's brow furrowed in confusion as he glanced around for Sharat, only to be informed by Devraj that he was on leave for a few days.

"But what about my code? Sharat never issued me one!"

Devraj reassured him with a grin, offering a solution to his predicament.

"That's because you weren't selling any policies. No problem at all. You can use my code for now; later, I'll transfer the policies to your code. Consider it a little boost to get you started."

Relieved and grateful, Arjun eagerly accepted Devraj's offer, his spirits buoyed by the prospect of continuing his success with the newfound support from his colleague.

9
Betrayal

As Arjun sat in the monthly review meeting, his anticipation was palpable. He worked tirelessly, putting in long hours and meticulously strategizing to meet his sales targets. Though he had yet to reach the lofty goal of 25 lakhs, he was certain Sharat would acknowledge his efforts and commend his dedication.

However, Arjun's confidence quickly turned to disbelief as the meeting progressed. His colleague, Devraj, was basking in the glory of achievements, receiving praise and accolades for surpassing his targets. Arjun's heart sank as he realized that his numbers were being displayed as almost negligible, a mere fraction of what he had actually accomplished.

Shock and dismay washed over Arjun as Sharat sternly directed sharp criticism at him, questioning his competence and dedication. Arjun felt paralyzed, unable to comprehend how his hard work had seemingly evaporated into thin air.

But amidst the confusion, a sudden realization dawned on him like a bolt from the blue. He remembered the transactions, the deals he had closed, all routed through

Devraj's code. It hit him like a betrayal, a bitter realization that Devraj had exploited his trust and taken advantage of his diligence.

At that moment, Arjun felt a mix of emotions—anger, betrayal, and profound disappointment. He couldn't fathom how Devraj could stoop so low, claiming Arjun's efforts as his own without a hint of remorse.

As the meeting continued, Arjun struggled to find his voice, torn between the urge to confront Devraj and the fear of further repercussions. The sense of injustice weighed heavy on his shoulders, leaving him reeling from the shock of being so blatantly taken advantage of.

As Arjun descended the staircase, his steps heavy with the weight of betrayal, he couldn't shake off the need to confront Devraj. With anger and disbelief swirling inside him, he approached Devraj, his voice trembling with the intensity of his emotions.

"Why didn't you tell Sharat it was my business?" Arjun's words tumbled out, laced with frustration and a sense of betrayal.

Devraj, with a smirk playing on his lips, responded in a shrewd tone that cut through Arjun like a knife. "Consider it a tribute for all the support you've received from me! You may call it Guru Dakshina," he said, his words dripping with arrogance and self-assurance.

Arjun's brows furrowed in disbelief, his disappointment becoming a simmering rage. How could Devraj justify stealing his hard-earned success as a mere "tribute"?

Arjun noticed the threat in Devraj's tone. With a clenched jaw, he mustered to warn Devraj, "I'll tell Sharat the truth, Devraj. You can't get away with this."

But Devraj's response was laced with a chilling confidence that sent shivers down Arjun's spine. "Think about it, Arjun," he said, his voice dripping with menace. "Who do you think Sharat will believe? A rookie like you, or the favorite Sales Manager?"

The realization hit Arjun like a punch to the gut. Devraj had positioned himself as untouchable, shielded by the favoritism of their superiors. It was a stark reminder of the harsh realities of office politics and power dynamics.

Frustration boiled within Arjun as he grappled with the unfairness of it all. He felt trapped, suffocated by the knowledge that speaking out against Devraj could spell disaster for his career within the company.

With a heavy heart and a cloud of disillusionment hanging over him, Arjun retreated, his spirit crushed by the weight of Devraj's manipulation and the harsh realities of corporate life.

The evening gloom enveloped the terrace as Arjun sat with Saurabh and Rishi, their minds burdened with the events of the day. Rishi's fury simmered visibly, and his fists clenched with the desire to confront Devraj head-on.

"I swear, I'll beat the shit out of that snake," Rishi spat out, his voice thick with anger as he vented his frustration.

Arjun, however, shook his head wearily, his disappointment evident in the slump of his shoulders. "I've had enough. It's not worth it. I'm quitting tomorrow," he said, his tone heavy with resignation.

Saurabh, the voice of reason among them, intervened gently. "Hold on, Arjun. Don't make rash decisions," he advised, his gaze steady through his spectacle glasses as he sought to calm the storm within his friend. "Things might seem bleak now, but trust me, the tables will turn someday. You'll have your moment."

As Arjun voiced his frustration, questioning why he should endure such hardships, "I have become the laughing stock of my office. Why should I endure this and that too at the cost of my dignity?"

Saurabh listened intently, his expression thoughtful. "I understand, Arjun," he began, his tone gentle yet firm. "But quitting won't solve the problem. You'll encounter people like Sharat and Devraj wherever you go. Learning to navigate these situations is crucial."

Arjun nodded slowly, acknowledging the truth in Saurabh's words. The realization that challenges were inevitable, no matter the workplace, settled heavily upon him."It's not just about today, Saurabh," Arjun murmured, his voice tinged with defeat. "I can't bear to see Devraj's face daily in the office, knowing what he's done. I'm tired, Saurabh. I'm just so tired."

Saurabh nodded understandingly, his expression reflecting the empathy he felt for his friend's plight. "I know, Arjun," he said softly, his words carrying the weight of their shared struggles. "This corporate world can be cruel, especially in sales. But remember, you're not alone in this. We're here for you, no matter what."

Reluctantly, Arjun agreed not to resign, his resolve bolstered by his friend's support. "Alright, I won't quit," he conceded, a hint of determination creeping into his voice. But what about Devraj's daily bullying? I can't bear that.``

Rishi intervened, offering a practical solution. "You don't have to, Arjun," he said reassuringly. "Just mark your attendance and head out into the field. Report back in the evening, and ignore Devraj completely while you're in the office. You already have your agent code now. So you can book your business. You don't need him!"

Arjun considered Rishi's suggestion, finding relief in avoiding Devraj's presence. It was a simple yet effective strategy to shield himself from further hurt.

As they sat in silence, their shared burden seemed to lighten slightly in the warmth of their friendship and solidarity. Amidst the chaos and betrayal, they found solace in each other's company. However, Arjun still dreaded the days to come. He had to start all over again now by building his base. His heart sank.

The following day marked the continuation of the saga. Arjun endured the relentless emotional torment day after day. Despite minimizing his time in the office, Devraj persisted in his bullying tactics, his malicious grins serving as a constant reminder of Arjun's ordeal.

Devraj's voice dripped with faux concern as he addressed Arjun, his tone oozing with shrewdness. "Hey Arjun, relax! Why are you getting so worked up? It's just business, after all."

Arjun's frustration boiled beneath the surface as he shot back, his voice tinged with resentment. "Easy for you to say. You stole my opportunities, reached the top, and left me in the dust."

Devraj shrugged nonchalantly, his smirk betraying his true intentions. "These things happen, Arjun. You need to learn to let go. You can always outperform me."

Arjun's frustration flared as he retorted, his words laced with bitterness. "That's not easy. You've sabotaged my chances, and now it'll take me ages to catch up.

"Oh come on forget about that. I have an offer for you. You can team up with me and then we can work together. I will give you all the support."

"You mean I shall become your sidekick. I do need support, but I won't trust you for it. And Sharat? Forget about it."

Devraj's response was dismissive, his indifference cutting through Arjun's resolve. "Suit yourself, mate. But don't you come calling on me when you are in trouble with Sharat," he said casually, his words a final jab in the ongoing battle of wills.

Arjun's onward journey was marked by a string of setbacks. Each evening, he faced Sharat's relentless scrutiny, responding with either zero results or negligible figures to the monthly target data (MTD) messages, bracing himself for the inevitable verbal lashing from his superior. Night after night, Arjun endured Sharat's tirades, absorbing the barrage of expletives with a heavy heart.

On one such evening, as Arjun listened to the familiar onslaught from Sharat, he reached his breaking point. "Arjun, you're utterly worthless as a sales manager," Sharat's voice thundered through the phone. "I'm thoroughly disappointed with HR. How could they hire someone as incompetent as you? If you can't succeed in Mumbai, you won't succeed anywhere. If you continue to underperform, I'll transfer you to the operations department. You'll be buried in paperwork..."

"Please do that, Sharat!" Arjun interjected, his voice firm with resolve. He was genuinely considering the prospect of transitioning to operations, unable to bear the weight of stress any longer. "I mean it, Sharat. I genuinely want to move to operations. Please transfer me there. I'm begging you."

Sharat, taken aback by Arjun's uncharacteristic defiance, was left speechless. He had anticipated Arjun to cower at the mere mention of a transfer to operations. Yet, Arjun's earnest plea conveyed a deeper longing for escape. Unable to muster a response, Sharat abruptly ended the call.

The following day, an email arrived from Priya, the HR manager, requesting Arjun's presence at 11 AM. The contents of the mail hinted at a significant development, leaving Arjun to ponder the uncertain future that awaited him.

10
Twisted Office Dynamics

———♡———

As Arjun made his way to the headquarters for his meeting with Priya, Rishi couldn't resist teasing him in his usual playful manner. "Life isn't fair is it?" he quipped, his grin widening mischievously. "I mean, there I am, just across the hall, and she invites you all the way from Ghatkopar for a chat?"

Arjun shrugged off Rishi's jests with a wry smile, but beneath his casual demeanor, there was a hint of unease. "I am damn sure it's Sharat's doing, maybe with a nudge from Devraj. After our little showdown yesterday, it wouldn't surprise me if he lodged a complaint. This could very well be my swan song at Zencorp," he admitted, a note of resignation in his voice.

Rishi's tone turned serious as he chided Arjun. "Why did you have to go macho on him? Sometimes it's better to swallow your pride and move on. But now, getting summoned by Priya the next day? That's too much of a coincidence. I smell trouble brewing, my friend."

As Arjun reached Priya's cabin and knocked on the glass door, he was surprised to see her emerge herself, greeting him with a warm smile. "Arjun, so nice to see you. Please, come in," she said, motioning for him to enter as she ushered him inside.

Seated across from each other, Priya poured coffee for them both, the atmosphere light and cheerful despite the formal setting. "How's everything going, Arjun?" she asked, her tone friendly yet professional.

Arjun smiled, appreciating Priya's welcoming demeanor. "Well, Priya Ma'am, it's been quite the rollercoaster ride lately," he admitted, a hint of wryness in his voice.

"Ah, I had a hunch. Can't say I'm shocked," Priya responded with a knowing smirk. "And please, it's just Priya. No need for the 'Ma'am'."

Priya nodded with a friendly smile, then reached for a file containing several papers. Arjun assumed it was his own file.

"So, Arjun, is this your first stint in Mumbai?" Priya inquired.

"Yes, Ma'am... I mean, yes, it is," Arjun replied, correcting himself with a chuckle.

Priya sat upright in her chair, her posture poised and attentive as she delicately broached the topic of Arjun's recent interaction with Sharat. There was a sense of quiet curiosity in her demeanor, a gentle probing masked by her calm and formal exterior.

"Arjun," she began, her voice soft but clear, "I've been briefed about your conversation with Sharat last night. It seems it was quite an... eventful exchange."

Her eyes, while maintaining a professional distance, held a glimmer of interest, as if she were eager to delve deeper into the dynamics at play. With each word, she carefully measured her tone, creating an atmosphere of exploration rather than interrogation.

"Well Priya! What you were briefed about is something I have been going through everyday!", said Arjun, his tone resigned to his fate.

"I'm intrigued to hear your perspective on the matter," Priya continued, her words flowing smoothly yet laden with a quiet intensity. "Could you walk me through your thoughts and feelings during the discussion?"

Despite the formality of the setting, there was an underlying warmth in Priya's demeanor, a subtle reassurance that Arjun's voice would be heard and respected. It was evident that she approached the conversation with a blend of professionalism and genuine curiosity, seeking to unravel the situation's complexities with grace and understanding.

As Arjun poured his heart out to Priya, recounting the events of the previous night with raw honesty, she listened intently, her gaze fixed on him with a compassionate understanding. Occasionally, she would jot down some notes, capturing key points of their discussion.

Once Arjun had shared all his thoughts, Priya leaned forward slightly, her demeanor shifting to that of a seasoned HR professional. With a gentle yet authoritative tone, she began to speak, her words carrying a soothing reassurance.

"Arjun," Priya began, her voice calm and steady, "I want you to know that I appreciate your honesty and candor. It's not easy to navigate challenges in the workplace, especially when emotions run high."

She paused, allowing her words to sink in before continuing. "I understand that this job may not be what you initially envisioned, but I want to assure you that you're not alone in this. We're here to support you every step of the way."

Priya's words were infused with genuine empathy as she sought to calm Arjun's anxieties and understand his perspective more deeply. With each sentence, she conveyed a sense of reassurance, painting a picture of a supportive workplace environment where Arjun's concerns would be addressed and his contributions valued.

"As we move forward, Arjun," Priya said, encouraging yet pragmatic, "let's work together to find a solution that aligns with your skills and aspirations. Your success is important to us, and we're committed to helping you thrive in your role here."

"But Priya, how am I supposed to succeed when the very individuals meant to mentor me are revealed to be deceitful? How can I face going to the same workplace where Devraj and Sharat relentlessly target me?" expressed Arjun, his distress evident in his words.

"Arjun, I understand the difficulties you're experiencing," Priya replied, her voice tinged with empathy. "But we must also remember that our company's primary goals are profits and bottom lines. Those who excel in delivering results often have more leeway. And Sharat and Devraj are the top performers in those benchmarks."

Arjun's disappointment was palpable. "So, it seems like inexperienced newcomers like me stand no chance against them. Why even recruit freshers if this is the case? It's all so overwhelming for me, and it's shattered my confidence," he lamented.

Priya's expression softened, her eyes conveying understanding. "I hear you, Arjun," she responded, her tone reassuring. "It's important to acknowledge these challenges. But remember, you're not alone in this. We're here to support you and help you overcome these obstacles." Priya nodded thoughtfully, her gaze steady as she shared her plan for Arjun. "That's why I have a different opportunity in mind for you," she said, her tone hopeful. "I'm transferring you to ZCP - Zen Corporate Park. It's the campus of our parent company, Zencorp Group. Your task will be to develop the business in the bustling campus, which houses over 25,000 employees, and promote our insurance offerings."

She continued, her voice brimming with determination. "It's unfortunate that employees of our own group aren't purchasing insurance from our sister concern. But it has been our fault. We have ignored that campus completely. Your mission will be to change that. Ensure that all group employees choose our insurance policies over those of other companies. Such a large congregation of business executives in one place presents you with a great opportunity."

Arjun's eyes widened in surprise at the unexpected turn of events. As Priya outlined the opportunity before him, a sense of excitement and purpose began to blossom within him.

"You will now report to Harish, the Branch Manager at the Navi Mumbai branch. But you will be posted at ZCP, and Your functions will be completely independent."

Arjun felt a wave of relief wash over him. The campus's location in Navi Mumbai meant he would be far removed from Devraj and Sharat. However, a new concern crept into his mind: What kind of boss would Harish, his new superior, turn out to be?

Priya seemed to sense his apprehension and reassured him, saying, "Don't worry, Arjun. I know you've had bitter experiences with Sharat, but Harish is nothing like them. You'll find him supportive and encouraging. He'll help you excel. The team out there is new and young."

Arjun's spirits lifted considerably at Priya's words. What he had anticipated to be a day of receiving his pink slip turned into a new beginning, filling him with hope and renewed enthusiasm.

As Arjun smiled, Priya noted the change in his demeanor. "I can see that you're happy," she remarked with a warm smile. "You can head to Navi Mumbai tomorrow and report to Harish. He'll provide you with all the details you need."

They shook hands, sealing the agreement, and Arjun left Priya's cabin with a grin spread across his face. Outside, Rishi greeted him, noticing the newfound cheer in Arjun's expression. "You're smiling, so I'm guessing you're not getting the boot," Rishi quipped.

Arjun chuckled, confirming Rishi's assumption. "You're right. I've been transferred to ZCP," he shared.

Rishi's eyes widened in surprise. "Wow, ZCP? That's a coveted place! People would kill to set foot on that campus. And you get to set up shop there?" he exclaimed incredulously.

Then, Rishi couldn't resist teasing Arjun about the attention Priya had given him. "Looks like Priya has taken quite a liking to you, huh? Giving you all that time and attention," he joked.

Priya was engrossed in her work on the laptop when Sharat strode into her cabin, his demeanor oozing with a sense of authority and arrogance. "Did he take the bait?" he inquired bluntly, his tone laced with impatience.

Priya looked up, her demeanor calm but cautious. "Have a little faith in my ability to handle things smoothly," she said, her tone steady yet determined. "He's taken the bait. Now, give the kid a chance."

Sharat scoffed dismissively. "He's useless to me," he declared bluntly. "I wanted him under Devraj's wing, following his directives. But he refuses. He's a liability, Priya. I want him gone."

"He is as good as gone! He will literally drown in ZCP. He won't be able to handle the pressures of that campus."

"Why transfer him, then?" Sharat asked, his tone dripping with sarcasm. "He is a bloody fresher. Why not just fire him?"

Priya's response was measured, her gaze steady as she met Sharat's gaze. "I don't believe in outright termination," she explained coolly. "I prefer to create circumstances that lead the individual to leave voluntarily. Remember it is a graveyard of Sales Managers. Firing someone reflects poorly on my position. It means my HR team is not good at recruiting quality staff. Besides, it's too much paperwork and takes some convincing to the Managing Director."

Sharat rolled his eyes, a cynical smirk playing on his lips. "The MD wants these freshers to be groomed like budding flowers. He sanctioned so much funds for those useless induction programs at Jodhpur. What a waste of time," he retorted derisively. "We should focus solely on profit-making."

Then, his eyes smoldering with rage, he seethed, "That damn rookie dared to defy me? Sharat Kabra? He has no idea who he's dealing with. I offered him a chance to join my team and earn a share of the commissions. But that fool just doesn't get it!"

"Hey, watch your language! You can't talk like that in the office. You have a terrible habit of being so coarse. Couldn't you have handled Arjun with a bit more tact?" Priya admonished, her tone firm but exasperated.

"Hey, Ms. HR Manager! Sales isn't all about sweet talk. It's about getting things done!" Sharat retorted sharply.

"Don't you dare raise your voice at me, Sharat! This isn't our living room!" Priya shot back, her patience wearing thin.

Sharat chuckled, but there was an edge to his laughter. "Oops! My mistake, dear. I wouldn't dream of yelling at my wife, even in our own living room!" he quipped.

Priya's expression softened slightly, a flicker of regret crossing her features as she murmured, "Perhaps it was a mistake for us to work in the same company. Husband and wife shouldn't mix business and personal life. Maybe I should propose a policy against it."

"Oh, I share your sentiment, my dear wife," Sharat replied with a sinister grin. "But you and I both know the riches we amass at Zencorp are simply too irresistible to pass up."

Their conversation was a dance of manipulation and power dynamics, each word carefully chosen to assert dominance and further their own agendas. In this cutthroat corporate world, compassion and empathy took a backseat to ruthless ambition and the relentless pursuit of financial gain. Arjun was a nobody to them. And it was at its full display in Priya's cabin.

11

The Haven

Today, Arjun was brimming with excitement as he anticipated a significant change. Finally liberated from the torment of Devraj and the constant cacophony created by Sharat, his life had been rendered almost unbearable by their presence. Their relentless pressure and stress had deprived him of sleep and caused him to shed a considerable amount of weight. Now, however, he was about to embark on a new chapter under the supervision of his new boss, Harish. Despite hearing positive remarks from Priya about Harish, Arjun couldn't shake off his lingering distrust and apprehension, a residue of the negative influence Sharat had exerted on his life thus far. As Arjun ventured to the Navi Mumbai branch, memories of his first encounter with the Ghatkopar branch flooded his mind, evoking a sense of nervous anticipation. However, upon arriving, he was pleasantly surprised. The Navi Mumbai office presented a striking contrast, with its spaciousness, ample lighting, and undeniable air of sophistication, a stark departure from the cramped confines of Ghatkopar. Arjun couldn't help but wonder if it was the vastness and relative tranquility of Navi Mumbai that contributed to the impressive aura of this branch.

As Arjun entered his new boss's cabin, he was greeted by an unexpected sight. Harish, his boss, was lounging comfortably in his chair, feet propped up on the desk, with a mischievous grin plastered across his face. The room was adorned with quirky decorations and amusing posters, giving off an air of casual playfulness.

"Ah, Arjun, my man!" Harish exclaimed, his tone light and jovial. "Welcome to the den of madness. Hope you've brought your sense of humor with you!"

Arjun couldn't help but chuckle at the sight before him. This was certainly not the stiff and formal atmosphere he had anticipated. Harish's easy going demeanor immediately put him at ease.

As Arjun settled into the conversation with Harish, the atmosphere was immediately charged with Harish's infectious humor.

"So, Arjun, tell me, have you discovered the secret to making insurance sales sound exciting yet?" Harish quipped, a mischievous glint in his eye.

Arjun chuckled, shaking his head. "Not quite, but I'm working on it."

Harish laughed, leaning back in his chair. "Ah, now that's the spirit! Who needs smoke and mirrors when you've got insurance policies, right?"

Their conversation quickly descended into a lighthearted exchange of anecdotes about the quirks and challenges of sales work at Zencorp. Harish regaled Arjun with humorous tales of attempting to sell insurance to skeptical clients, punctuating each story with his trademark wit and sarcasm.

"Ah, the glamorous life of an insurance salesman," Harish joked, rolling his eyes dramatically. "I tell you, Arjun, it's a wonder we're not all millionaires by now with the sheer excitement of it all."

Arjun couldn't help but laugh at Harish's playful mockery of their line of work. Despite the inherent challenges, Harish's irreverent humor made the prospect of diving into the world of insurance sales seem oddly appealing.

"So there I was, trying to explain the intricacies of life insurance to this guy, right in the middle of the bustling street market," Harish recounted, a grin spreading across his face. "And just when I thought I was making progress, he looks me dead in the eye and says, 'Bhai, if I die, my problems will die with me. Who's going to worry about life insurance then?"

Arjun burst into laughter, picturing the absurdity of the situation. Harish's knack for storytelling never failed to entertain.

Arjun chuckled at Harish's anecdote and then shared one of his own. "Tell me about it," he said with a grin. "I once went to sell insurance to a guy who ended up pitching me his own ULIP plan!"

Harish burst into laughter, thoroughly entertained by Arjun's story. "Now, that's what I call turning the tables! You've got to appreciate the entrepreneurial spirit, even if it catches you off guard."

After a moment of shared laughter, Harish leaned in, adopting a more serious tone. "But you see, Arjun, that's the thing about sales. It's unpredictable. You never know what curveballs you'll encounter. The key is to roll with the punches, adapt to the situation, and always keep a sense of humor about it."

Arjun nodded in agreement, appreciating the insight. As they continued their conversation, he realized that there was much to learn from Harish's blend of humor and wisdom. Armed with these lessons, he knew that working under Harish was going to be anything but boring.

Harish leaned back in his chair, a smirk playing on his lips. "So, Arjun, you get the crown jewel! The ZCP campus is your workplace," he declared a hint of amusement in his voice.

With a knowing look, Harish painted a vivid picture of what selling insurance at ZCP would entail. "Picture this," he began, gesturing with his hands for emphasis. "You'll be stepping into the world of suave executives, where English is the lingua franca and Hindi or any vernacular language might as well be ancient hieroglyphics. Twenty-five thousand of them in one campus!"

Leaning in, he whispered, "And those with spacious, solitary cabins? The corporate elites! Rumor has it they even go to the toilet in their SUVs!"

Arjun couldn't help but chuckle at the image Harish painted. The contrast between his previous experiences and the upscale world of ZCP was stark indeed.

"But here's the thing," Harish continued, his tone turning more serious. "Don't let the shiny exterior fool you. Beneath all the glitz and glamour, these executives have the same concerns as anyone else. They worry about their families, their futures, their security."

He leaned back again, a thoughtful expression on his face. "Your job, Arjun, is to connect with them on a human level. Show them that insurance isn't just about fancy policies and big words. It's about peace of mind, security, and taking care of their cars, their plush bungalows, and assets that they love the most."

Arjun nodded, taking in Harish's words. "You know, Arjun, we've had our fair share of experienced sales managers handling the business of ZCP. But, most of them couldn't handle it. Many of them ended up resigning."

He went on to explain the challenges of selling insurance in such an environment. "It's not just about the language barrier or the lavish lifestyles," he said, shaking his head. "The truth is, these corporate bigwigs are a tough crowd to crack. They're skeptical, discerning, and they've heard every sales pitch in the book."

Harish paused, letting his words sink in before continuing. "And let's not forget the competition. Every insurance agent in the city is vying for their attention. You've got to find a way to stand out from the crowd, to offer something truly valuable and compelling."

Arjun nodded, feeling a sense of both trepidation and determination. "I'll try my best, Boss!"

"Now here's the deal, Arjun. Earlier the Sales Manager dealt with the business from the Navi Mumbai office. But you'll be stationed there at ZCP," he began, his voice firm. "And you won't be alone. You have two Customer Service Officers, or CSO in short, whose sole job will be to run around, fetching leads, collecting cheques, filling forms, and whatever else you need."

He continued, "There's also a girl who handles operations. She's crucial. You see, the executives on this campus don't like to wait. Once they write that cheque for the premium payment, you've got to get it to her immediately, she'll work her magic on the centralized software, print the policy document, and you need to deliver it to them pronto before they even think about changing their minds."

Harish emphasized the importance of efficiency and timeliness in this environment. "Time is of the essence here, Arjun. These executives move fast, and we've got to keep up.

So, make sure you've got everything streamlined and ready to go. One slip-up, and we could lose a valuable client and our jobs!"

Arjun nodded, taking in the gravity of his new responsibilities. Selling insurance at ZCP was going to be a whole new ballgame, but with Harish's guidance and the support of his team, he felt ready to rise to the challenge.

Harish's expression turned serious as he leaned in to impart a word of caution to Arjun. "Now, Arjun, I need you to be a bit cautious about those two CSOs, I mentioned. Their names are Rajan and Ganesh. They may seem harmless, but they're actually quite shrewd. They have a knack for avoiding work and prefer to roam around the campus instead of fulfilling their duties."

He continued, his voice tinged with concern, "These peons have been known to make life difficult for the sales manager stationed here. Their lack of productivity and constant evasion of responsibilities have frustrated many a sales managers to the point of quitting."

Arjun, puzzled by the situation, posed a question to Harish. "Why not just fire them and bring in more productive replacements?" he asked, genuinely curious.

Harish sighed, understanding Arjun's perspective. "I've thought about it," he replied, a hint of frustration in his voice. "But it's not that simple. These peons, as troublesome as they may be, have their own connections and networks within the campus. They know the ins and outs, the key players, the unofficial rules."

He paused, choosing his words carefully. "Firing them could disrupt the delicate balance we've managed to maintain there. Plus, finding replacements who are equally familiar with the campus and its dynamics would take time and effort we can't afford to spare. When they are gone there would be a vacuum in the campus. And any executive could straight away call the MD about this lack of service on the campus. And that would mean the pink slip for me."

Harish leaned back, his expression thoughtful. "Arjun, we have to work with what we have and find ways to mitigate the challenges they pose. It's not ideal, but it's the reality of the situation."

Arjun nodded, beginning to grasp the complexities of the situation. "I see," he said, absorbing Harish's explanation. "I'll do my best to manage them."

"Good to hear that! Now you go and take a seat in the office. Relax for a while and spend time in the office. Meet the staff. In the evening I will take you to ZCP and give you a tour. You then start your work posted from there tomorrow onwards. But remember to report to me here at least twice a week, preferably in the evenings before you leave for home."

"Of course, Harish," Arjun responded, starting to make his way out. However, before he could leave, Harish halted him and inquired about how he found himself in this particular situation. Arjun proceeded to recount the ordeal he endured at the hands of Devraj and Sharat, detailing how their actions had led him to seek help from Priya, who subsequently arranged his transfer to this new position.

"I get it now! But unveiling Sharat's misdeeds to Priya was akin to complaining about a thief to a dacoit!" Harish exclaimed, his eyes gleaming with intensity.

"What on earth does that mean?" Arjun asked, his surprise evident.

"Don't you know?" Harish whispered, his voice tinged with suspense. "Sharat and Priya, they're husband and wife!"

12

The Hell!

As Harish and Arjun swiped their IDs to enter the ZCP campus, Arjun's eyes widened in awe as he took in the sight of the sprawling campus and the towering glass buildings that dominated the skyline. The sunlight danced off the reflective surfaces, casting a shimmering glow over the meticulously landscaped grounds.

The main building, a sleek skyscraper of steel and glass, rose majestically into the sky, its facade adorned with the ZCP logo. Surrounding it were several smaller buildings, each with its own unique architectural flair, connected by covered walkways and lush green spaces.

Arjun couldn't help but feel a sense of excitement and anticipation as he stepped onto the campus, his gaze darting from one impressive structure to another. The sheer scale of the place was staggering, and he couldn't help but marvel at the thought of the countless opportunities that lay within its walls.

Harish, noticing Arjun's amazement, offered a reassuring smile. "Quite a change from selling door to door in the dirt-ridden streets of Mumbai right? Many experienced Sales Managers would kill to be in here," he said, his tone tinged with pride. "You're getting this opportunity only three months into your career. Consider yourself lucky."

Arjun nodded, feeling a rush of adrenaline. As he looked around at the impressive surroundings, he couldn't help but feel excited for what lay ahead.

As they both entered one of the buildings, Arjun noticed two men approaching him. Dressed in formal attire, their demeanor exuded a sense of authority, yet they appeared somewhat out of place amidst the corporate ambiance. They came forward and greeted Harish warmly, their attention seemingly diverted from Arjun. These were Rajan and Ganesh, the CSOs. Harish engaged in a brief conversation with them before they all proceeded into the building.

Inside, they stepped into a vast hall lined with hundreds of cubicles, all neatly arranged in rows. Glass cabins dotted the periphery, likely reserved for managers and executives. The atmosphere was bustling with activity, the air punctuated by the sounds of keyboards clicking, printers humming, and phones ringing. Despite the apparent chaos, there was an underlying sense of order and efficiency.

However, what struck Arjun the most was the conspicuous absence of conversation. Despite the cacophony of technological sounds filling the space, not a single word was exchanged between colleagues. Instead, everyone seemed engrossed in their tasks, their focus undivided as they diligently worked away.

The scene painted a picture of intense concentration and dedication, where every individual was fully immersed in their responsibilities. It was a silent symphony of productivity, where the rhythm of work echoed through the halls, uninterrupted by the noise of conversation.

In the remote corner of that bustling hall, a smaller cubicle stood apart, designated for the Zencorp Insurance team. Seated at the desk within was a young woman named Charu, her fingers dancing across the keyboard as she typed with practiced ease. Upon noticing Harish and Arjun's arrival, she rose from her seat with a warm smile, addressing them both respectfully as "sir."

Harish introduced Arjun to Charu, and in turn, to Rajan and Ganesh, the CSOs. Charu greeted Arjun with genuine warmth, extending a welcoming hand and expressing her pleasure at meeting him. Despite her youthfulness, there was an air of professionalism about her demeanor, indicative of her readiness to take on the responsibilities of her role.

However, as the introductions unfolded, Arjun couldn't help but sense a subtle shift in the atmosphere. While Charu's reception was cordial, Rajan and Ganesh's responses were noticeably restrained. Their expressions conveyed a hint of disapproval, and there was a distinct lack of enthusiasm in their greetings. It was evident that they harbored reservations about Arjun's presence on the campus, perhaps viewing him as an interloper encroaching upon their territory.

As Harish led Arjun further into the cubicle area, he leaned in to explain the roles of their colleagues. "Arjun, Charu here looks after the operations. She's quite adept with our company's official online software portal and can whip up policy documents in no time," he said, gesturing towards Charu, who nodded in affirmation.

Arjun nodded in acknowledgment, impressed by Charu's proficiency. "That's great to know, Charu. I'm sure we'll be working closely together," he said with a friendly smile.

Harish then turned his attention to Rajan and Ganesh, who were standing nearby. "Rajan and Ganesh know every corner of the campus," he explained, nodding towards them.

Rajan and Ganesh acknowledged the introduction with a curt nod, their expressions guarded.

"And now," Harish continued, his tone taking on a more serious note, "Arjun will be looking after affairs here in ZCP, and all of you will report to him."

At Harish's announcement, Rajan and Ganesh's faces visibly fell, their expressions turning sour with disdain towards Arjun. There was an unmistakable tension in the air as they exchanged glances, their displeasure at the news evident.

Arjun sensed the shift in atmosphere and exchanged a brief glance with Harish, silently acknowledging the challenge ahead. It was clear that his new position would not come without its share of resistance, but he was determined to earn the respect of his colleagues and prove himself worthy of the responsibility entrusted to him.

It took a while as Harish took stock of the work from Charu, Rajan, and Ganesh, he glanced at his watch and sighed. "It's time for us to head out," he announced, straightening up.

Arjun nodded in understanding, realizing that the day was drawing to a close. Turning to Charu, Rajan, and Ganesh, Harish addressed them collectively. "Keep everything on track, everyone. Arjun will be taking over from tomorrow," he informed them, his tone firm yet reassuring.

Rajan and Ganesh exchanged a glance, their expressions still tinged with reluctance.

Then, focusing his attention on Arjun, Harish spoke again. "I'll drop you off at the nearest local train station so you can head home," he offered kindly. "Start coming here from tomorrow."

Arjun nodded, expressing his gratitude once again. With a final exchange of farewells, Harish led Arjun out of the building, ready to embark on the next phase of his journey at ZCP.

***

"No way! Priya and Sharat? Married?" Rishi's reaction was one of shock and disbelief. He exclaimed, his eyes wide with incredulity.

Arjun nodded solemnly, confirming the unexpected news.

Saurabh furrowed his brow, pondering over Arjun's previous complaints about Sharat to Priya. "So, you were venting about Sharat to Priya, in her office, and she actually turned out to be his wife?" he asked, a hint of amusement in his voice.

Arjun grimaced, feeling a twinge of embarrassment at the realization. "Yeah, looks like it," he admitted sheepishly.

Rishi let out a sigh, shaking his head in disbelief. "Man, I can't believe Priya is married. I am so heartbroken!" he exclaimed, unable to contain his astonishment. Then, with a hint of humor, he added, "How on earth did she end up marrying him? She is such a doll! He looks like a boiled egg!"

The absurdity of the situation prompted laughter from all three friends, momentarily lightening the mood despite the unexpected revelation. As they continued to discuss the news, Arjun couldn't help but marvel at the unpredictable twists and turns of life, realizing that sometimes reality truly is stranger than fiction.

As they sat on the terrace enjoying their beers, Saurabh's tone took on a more serious note as he leaned in towards Arjun. "You really need to take this seriously now," he urged, his expression grave. "It's apparent that Priya transferred you to ZCP at the behest of Sharat. It seems like they're hoping you'll get frustrated and resign."

Arjun's brows furrowed as he processed Saurabh's words, the implications sinking in. "But why would they do that?" he asked, a hint of confusion in his voice.

Saurabh sighed, shaking his head. "Who knows? Maybe they see you as a threat or nuisance, or maybe they just want to make life difficult for you," he speculated. "Either way, you need to be cautious and handle this situation carefully."

Arjun nodded slowly, a sense of determination settling over him. "I won't let them push me out without a fight," he vowed, his resolve firm.

Rishi, who had been listening intently, chimed in with words of encouragement. "That's the spirit, Arjun! Don't let them get the better of you," he said, offering his support.

With renewed determination, Arjun prepared himself for the challenges that lay ahead, knowing that he would need to navigate the complexities of office politics with skill and perseverance. As the conversation continued, he felt a sense of gratitude for the unwavering support of his friends, knowing that they would be there for him every step of the way.

As Arjun arrived punctually at the ZCP campus the next day, he found the cubicle deserted, devoid of any signs of activity. Patiently, he waited, the minutes ticking by slowly. Half an hour later, Charu appeared, her demeanor tinged with a hint of trepidation upon seeing Arjun.

"Why the surprise?" Arjun inquired, his voice calm.

Charu, her eyes betraying her unease, explained, "We've never had a sales manager stationed here before. So, the concept of punctuality was a bit of a shock."

Arjun nodded understandingly, acknowledging the unusual circumstances. Turning his attention to the whereabouts of Rajan and Ganesh, he asked Charu about their tardiness.

"They arrive whenever they please," she responded, a hint of resignation in her voice.

As they settled into their work, Charu busied herself with the computer while Arjun absorbed the environment, pondering the lackadaisical attitude of his colleagues.

Around 11 AM, the atmosphere in the hall shifted as Rajan and Ganesh strolled in, their presence marked by an air of nonchalance. Arjun wasted no time in addressing their tardiness, his tone firm yet composed.

"Good morning, Rajan, Ganesh. You both arrived quite late. Any reason for the delay?"

Rajan shrugged casually, a smirk playing on his lips. "Oh, Boss, you know how it is. Just taking our time. No rush, right?"

Ganesh chimed in with a careless shrug, echoing Rajan's sentiment. "Yes, Boss. We don't really stick to schedules around here. It's more of a go-with-the-flow kind of vibe. It's the norm around here."

Arjun's brow furrowed slightly, his tone firm as he tried to reason with them. "But punctuality is essential for the smooth functioning of our team. We need to be accountable for our time and commitments."

Rajan waved off his concerns with a dismissive gesture. "Relax, Boss. We get the job done eventually. What's the big deal?"

Ganesh nodded in agreement, already edging towards the exit. "Exactly. You just chill out, boss. Leave the business to us."

As they nonchalantly made their way out of the hall, Arjun couldn't help but feel a sense of exasperation wash over him. Their indifference towards punctuality grated against his principles, leaving him with a lingering sense of disrespect hanging in the air.

As he simmered with frustration over Rajan and Ganesh's lackadaisical attitude, Charu approached him with a calming presence.

"Sir, please don't let their behavior get to you too much," she said soothingly. "They've always been like this. It might take some time for them to adjust to your management style."

Arjun nodded, appreciating Charu's perspective. "You're right, Charu. I suppose I'll have to be patient and give them some time to adapt."

With a shared understanding, they redirected their focus to their work. Arjun's curiosity piqued, he turned to Charu, gesturing towards the computer screen.

"What are you working on?" he inquired, leaning in to get a closer look.

Charu smiled, eager to share her tasks with Arjun. "I'm using this online software to develop and print insurance policies on our company letterhead. It streamlines the process and ensures consistency in our documents."

Intrigued, Arjun observed as Charu navigated through the software, explaining its functionalities and benefits. As she demonstrated the system, Arjun's mind churned with ideas on how to optimize their workflow.

"So, after the policies are generated here," Arjun summarized, "Rajan and Ganesh physically deliver them to the clients?"

Charu nodded, confirming Arjun's understanding. "Yes, that's correct. They handle the distribution while I manage the backend operations. While outside a policy takes a week to be delivered, here at ZCP, we instantly print and deliver the policy without any delay."

Feeling restless with a salesman's instinct to keep moving, Arjun decided to explore the ZCP campus. As he wandered through the halls and corridors, his keen observation didn't escape the palpable atmosphere of tension that seemed to envelop the entire workplace.

Everywhere he looked, faces were drawn with stress, brows furrowed in concentration, and shoulders tense with the weight of their responsibilities. Despite his attempts to engage with his colleagues, offering friendly greetings and his business card, he was met with indifference. No one spared a moment to reciprocate his gestures or express any interest in connecting.

Arjun couldn't help but feel a sense of bewilderment creeping over him. Why was the work environment at ZCP so suffocatingly laden with stress and pressure? What had caused this pervasive atmosphere of tension to settle over the campus like a thick fog?

Pausing in his tracks, Arjun took a moment to reflect on his observations. Perhaps the absence of a relaxed and welcoming atmosphere was contributing to the overall sense of disengagement among the employees.

As the days stretched into a week, Arjun found himself increasingly disenchanted with the stagnant atmosphere that pervaded the halls of ZCP. Despite his best efforts to inject enthusiasm and productivity into his role as a sales manager, he found himself met with a disheartening lack of opportunity and engagement.

Each morning seemed to blend seamlessly into the next, with Arjun arriving at the campus only to be greeted by the same dreary tableau of stressed faces and empty corridors. The absence of leads to pursue left him feeling aimless and unfulfilled, his eagerness to make an impact waning with each passing day.

Rajan and Ganesh remained obstinately indifferent to Arjun's attempts to connect, their apathy serving as a constant reminder of his isolation within the team. Their casual disregard for his presence only added to his growing sense of frustration and disillusionment.

As he sat alone in his cubicle, the minutes ticking by in agonizing monotony, Arjun couldn't shake the feeling of being adrift in a sea of inertia. Despite his best intentions, it seemed that there was little he could do to break free from the suffocating grip of boredom and stagnation that had taken hold of ZCP.

In the quiet of the late hours of the Navi Mumbai office, he tried to find some solace in the company of Harish, seeking counsel in the face of the challenges that had plagued him since his arrival at ZCP. He poured out his frustrations to Harish, his words heavy with the weight of disillusionment.

"I just don't understand it, Harish," Arjun began, his tone tinged with exasperation. "No matter what I do, I can't seem to generate any new leads here. And Rajan and Ganesh, they're completely unresponsive to any attempts at collaboration."

Harish listened intently, his brow furrowed in thought as he pondered Arjun's predicament. After a moment of contemplation, he offered his insight with a sagely nod.

"You see, Arjun, the business in ZCP has been stagnant for quite some time now," Harish explained, his voice tinged with resignation. "No one really bothers about it because it's not growing. But if it were to start growing, then perhaps people would start taking notice."

Arjun nodded, absorbing Harish's words as he contemplated the magnitude of the untapped potential within the vast campus of 25,000 employees.

"But how do I kickstart that growth?" Arjun questioned, his gaze searching Harish's for answers.

Harish leaned forward, his expression grave as he shared his insights. "You'll have to find innovative ways to generate more leads, Arjun. And as for Rajan and Ganesh, their motivations lie in their fixed salaries and the variable pay they receive based on business generated."

A flicker of realization illuminated Arjun's features as he connected the dots. "But they're not generating any business at all," he exclaimed, frustration creeping into his voice. "I have never seen them bringing any duly filled application form and premium cheque. All they seem to do is loiter around the campus."

Harish nodded knowingly. "Then perhaps it's time to dig deeper, Arjun. Use the software to find out what business is being reported. It might shed some light on the situation."

"I will sit with Charu on it tomorrow."

The next day Arjun sought the assistance of Charu, the ever-reliable source of information. Requesting a list of all policies generated in the past six months, Arjun eagerly awaited the results, his mind abuzz with anticipation.

As Charu handed over the printed list, Arjun wasted no time in delving into the data, his eyes scanning each entry with meticulous attention to detail. It wasn't long before a pattern began to emerge, one that sent a shiver of realization down Arjun's spine.

"Charu, what does 'R' signify?" Arjun inquired, his voice betraying a hint of urgency.

"R stands for renewals. These are policies that have been renewed before or on their expiration date."

Arjun's brows furrowed in contemplation as the implications of this revelation sank in. "So, almost 90% of the policies generated are not new but renewals of already existing policies?" he mused aloud.

Charu nodded solemnly, confirming Arjun's suspicions. "Yes, Sir. The software automatically sends an email to the client to remind them of renewal. When they renew their policies it reflects here. Most of the clients do it instantly because they do not want to take the effort to find a new insurer."

Suddenly, everything clicked into place for Arjun as he made a startling realization. "So that's why our business here hasn't been growing. And I see that Rajan and Ganesh are getting commission on these renewals," he exclaimed, a note of frustration creeping into his voice. "So that's where their paycheck comes from. They're earning commission without putting in any effort at all."

"It seems so, sir", Charu exclaimed, a little embarrassed for not knowing the obvious fact till now.

With a sense of righteous indignation burning within him, Arjun made a decision then and there. "It's time to put an end to this nonsense," he declared, his tone resolute. "From now on, Rajan and Ganesh will only receive commission on new business generated. No more free lunches on auto-renewals."

Charu looked at Arjun with admiration, her eyes reflecting her newfound respect for his leadership. "That's a bold move, Sir," she remarked, her voice filled with admiration. "But is it right to take them head-on?"

"No need to tell them. I will fix this glitch in the software. Payday is near. They will see that their commission is zero this time. Let them come to me with their grievance."

As payday arrived, Arjun braced himself for the inevitable confrontation with Rajan and Ganesh. Sure enough, they stormed into the cubicle with a palpable sense of fury radiating from their every step. Ignoring Arjun completely, they directed their anger towards Charu, laying the blame for their discontent squarely at her feet.

"You must have messed up in the software," Rajan accused, his voice laced with venom. "We didn't receive any commission for this month."

Before Charu could respond, Arjun stepped forward, his expression steely with resolve. "It wasn't Charu who made the changes," he interjected, his voice cutting through the tension in the air. "It was me."

The revelation hung heavy in the air as Rajan and Ganesh turned their wrath towards Arjun, their eyes ablaze with indignation. Arjun stood his ground, unwavering in his decision to reform the commission structure.

"No free lunches. From now on, you'll only receive a commission on new business generated," Arjun declared firmly, his tone brooking no argument.

The announcement sparked an immediate backlash from Rajan and Ganesh, their protests ringing out in the cramped confines of the cubicle. They argued vehemently against Arjun's decision.

"Young boys like you won't be able to handle the campus business at all!" Rajan spat, his words dripping with contempt. "The business here runs because of us, not because of you."

"We shall see," undeterred by their threats, Arjun stood firm in his resolve, refusing to back down in the face of their intimidation tactics. Rajan and Ganesh stormed out of the cubicle in a flurry of frustration, "We've been bringing in business for years," Rajan protested, his tone bordering on defiance. "Don't expect us to work for nothing?"

Arjun remained steadfast in his belief that change was necessary for the growth and success of the team, no matter the challenges that lay ahead.

As the tension settled in the cubicle after Rajan and Ganesh's departure, Charu's worried gaze met Arjun's determined stare. Sensing her concern, she voiced her apprehensions about the practicalities of running the campus business without the support of Rajan and Ganesh.

"How will things run now, Sir?" she asked, her voice tinged with uncertainty. "The campus is too big and vast for you to handle alone."

Arjun's expression remained resolute as he reassured her, "I'll manage somehow, Charu. But I won't tolerate being talked down upon by non-performers and bullies. Now tell me. How does someone on the campus who needs insurance contact us?"

Charu highlighted a critical issue. "Clients usually contact Rajan and Ganesh directly," she explained. "And you just shooed them away!"

"Oh dear!" Arjun was taken aback. He hadn't given this a thought. But then he regained his composure. "Isn't there a centralized number for clients to reach out to us?"

Charu nodded, acknowledging his observation. "There is a landline, but its number isn't known to anyone outside this cubicle."

"Rajan and Ganesh must have deliberately done that. So as to create full dependency on them. How can we ensure that this information reaches all employees on the campus?" he pondered aloud.

Charu's eyes lit up with an idea. "We could include it in the weekly mailer sent to all employees," she suggested.

"Great! And whom do I talk to for that?"

"Mr. Brajesh, the head of this department. Right down the hall!"

With a plan forming in his mind, Arjun nodded appreciatively. "Thank you, Charu. I'll make sure to follow up on this," he assured her, his determination unwavering as he prepared to tackle the challenges ahead.

13

Inside the tiger's den

As Arjun ambled through the campus, the rhythm of his steps was suddenly disrupted by a jarring blast of sound. A hooter pierced the air, its shrill tone commanding attention. Perplexed, Arjun surveyed his surroundings, only to find the once-bustling pavements frozen in place. Not a soul dared to tread the road, every foot firmly planted in a strange tableau of stillness.

His curiosity piqued, Arjun followed the collective gaze skyward, searching for the source of the disturbance. A sleek silhouette materialized against the azure canvas above—a chopper, descending with a graceful swoop onto the campus grounds. The thrum of its rotors drowned out all other sounds, casting a spell of anticipation over the mesmerized onlookers.

Minutes trickled by like fleeting seconds until, finally, the chopper settled onto the earth with a gentle thud. In its wake, an orange blur streaked through the campus, slicing through the air with effortless agility. As quickly as it had appeared, the enigmatic imported car, one that Arjun had not seen even in movies, vanished from sight, leaving behind a wake of wonder and speculation.

With the spell broken, the hooter sounded once more, releasing the captive populace from its temporary stasis. Arjun, still reeling from the spectacle, sought solace in his cubicle, eager to unravel the mystery. There, he shared his tale with Charu, who offered a cryptic explanation.

"It's the MD," she revealed, her voice tinged with reverence. "He descends upon the campus in his chopper every fortnight, a symbol of his authority and efficiency. No one is allowed and no one dares to cross his path—not when his time is deemed sacrosanct, his movements a matter of security."

Arjun's mind buzzed with intrigue as he pondered the implications. Here he was, dreaming of a modest car purchase that would require years of scrimping and saving, while the MD effortlessly commandeered a luxury vehicle for mere moments of transit from his heliport to his office once every fortnight. The irony was not lost on him, prompting a wry chuckle amidst the enigma that shrouded ZCP's upper echelons.

Despite Arjun's persistent efforts to meet Mr. Brajesh, the head of the department, his attempts were continually thwarted by the constant stream of visitors filling Brajesh's cabin. Each time Arjun approached, the glass door offered only fleeting glimpses of figures engrossed in discussions, leaving him unable to catch Brajesh alone. Despite his vigilance and strategic timing, Arjun's efforts proved fruitless, with frustration gnawing at his resolve as he reluctantly conceded defeat. Yet, undeterred by this setback, Arjun remained resolute, determined to find alternative ways to navigate the intricate web of relationships within the campus.

As the phone rang, Arjun's heart raced with anticipation. Finally, Brajesh answered the call, his voice sharp and authoritative. Arjun took a deep breath, steeling himself as he introduced himself.

"Hello, Mr. Brajesh. This is Arjun," he began, only to be interrupted by an unexpected response.

"I know who you are, Arjun," Brajesh interjected curtly, his tone brimming with irritation. "I've seen you peeking into my cabin multiple times instead of simply coming in. What's the matter? Can't you muster the courage to approach me directly?"

Taken aback by Brajesh's harsh rebuke, Arjun struggled to find the words to respond. Before he could formulate a reply, Brajesh continued his tirade, his words cutting through the air like a whip.

"A cowardly man like you has no place as an insurance salesman," Brajesh declared, his voice dripping with disdain. "If you can't even face me directly, how do you expect to handle the challenges of this job?"

With those cutting words, Brajesh abruptly ended the call, leaving Arjun stunned and disheartened. As he processed the encounter, a mix of frustration and determination welled up within him. He was completely shaken up and his confidence had taken a deep dive into the Mariana Trench.

Arjun, frustrated by being bashed up over the phone turned to Charu for guidance, he posed a pointed question: "Charu, I think I should contact his superior. To whom does Mr. Brajesh report?"

Charu, ever the reliable source of information, responded without hesitation. "Mr. Brajesh reports directly to the Managing Director."

Arjun's eyebrows shot up in surprise, his initial shock quickly giving way to a sense of incredulity. "The Managing Director? Oh dear," he repeated incredulously. "Surely, I can't approach the MD to address something as trivial as sending emailers to employees. I can't approach the MD anyway. I am too small a fish."

"Absolutely, Sir. However, I strongly suggest steering clear of Mr. Brajesh's office for the time being," advised Charu.

"Agreed," Arjun concurred.

He headed to the cafeteria for his lunch. While he was barely able to swallow his dosa and vada, Rajan and Ganesh approached his table, resembling two unruly dinosaurs.

"So, we heard you received a scolding from Mr. Brajesh himself!" Rajan remarked.

"Do you really believe you can impress him with your MBA knowledge straight out of the textbooks?" Ganesh added with a smirk.

"Boss, we've spent three years on this campus and haven't even dared to approach the fourth cubicle near his office. And here you are, thinking you can just call and schedule an appointment," Ganesh teased Arjun.

"Face it, you won't survive here. Consider requesting a transfer or something," Rajan suggested. "Or if you prefer, we can revert to the old ways. You sit back, relax, and report the business as usual. No one will bother you, as no one really cares about business around here. You can just chill out with us," Rajan continued.

Feeling defeated, Arjun chose not to respond to their taunts, unwilling to reveal his vulnerability. He silently finished his meal and retreated to his cubicle.

14

Retreat

As customary on a weekend evening, Arjun, Rishi, and Saurabh sat together, their glasses clinking with each toast. Yet, the atmosphere was tinged with frustration and despondency. Arjun's furrowed brows betrayed his inner turmoil as he swirled the amber liquid in his glass, the ice cubes clinking softly.

"I just don't get it, guys," Arjun muttered, his voice heavy with frustration. "No matter what I do, nothing moves! It's like banging my head against a brick wall."

Rishi nodded solemnly, taking a sip from his drink. "Tell me about it. I thought my brilliant sales strategies would pick up some momentum by now, but it's like I am stuck in quicksand."

Arjun, leaning back in his chair, sighed deeply. "The pressure and stress is getting unbearable. If we don't turn things around soon, we'll be out on the streets before we know it."

Rishi leaned forward, his eyes glinting with determination. "Maybe it's time we start looking elsewhere. There's only so much we can do here."

Saurabh nodded, a spark of hope igniting in his eyes. "I've already started scouting for opportunities. There's a company I've applied to, and I can forward both of your resumes if you're interested."

Arjun's spirits lifted at the prospect, a glimmer of optimism breaking through the clouds of despair. "Really? That would be amazing, Saurabh. Anything to get out of this rut."

Rishi raised his glass in a toast, a faint smile playing on his lips. "To new beginnings and better fortunes. May this be the start of something great."

As they clinked their glasses together, the weight of their troubles momentarily lifted, replaced by a shared sense of hope and possibility in the midst of their drunken conversation.

Monsoons arrived with the force of a symphony, a cacophony of droplets dancing upon the city's streets, rooftops, and leaves. It painted the cityscape in shades of gray, washing away the dust and grime of urban life, revealing the hidden beauty beneath. The air became heavy with the scent of wet earth, and the sound of raindrops created a soothing melody that serenaded the soul.

Despite its enchanting allure, Mumbai's rain was a double-edged sword, bringing both delight and despair. For some, it offered respite from the scorching heat and a chance to revel in the cool embrace of nature. But for others, particularly those living in low-lying areas or makeshift shelters, it spelled disaster, flooding streets and homes, disrupting daily life, and posing health risks.

As Arjun navigated through the deluge, his steps were weighed down by the relentless downpour, and he felt a creeping sense of weakness gnawing at his bones. The rain beat against his umbrella like a relentless drum, soaking through his clothes despite his attempts to shield himself. Every step was a struggle against the onslaught of water, his vision blurred by the curtain of rain that surrounded him.

Finally reaching home, Arjun shed his drenched clothes, the chill of the rain clinging to his skin like a persistent shadow. As he tried to warm himself, he found that his shivering intensified, his teeth chattering uncontrollably. A feverish haze descended upon him, his body wracked with pain and exhaustion.

Rishi and Saurabh, alarmed by Arjun's deteriorating condition, wasted no time in rushing him to the nearest doctor. After a series of tests, the diagnosis was clear: malaria, a cruel twist of fate amidst the monsoon season. Arjun was prescribed medication and instructed to rest for at least five days, his body too weak to withstand the demands of daily life.

Confined to his bed, Arjun's days blurred into a haze of discomfort and suffering. The fever raged within him like a relentless inferno, leaving him drenched in sweat and delirious with pain. Every movement was an agony, every breath a struggle against the relentless onslaught of illness.

As the days passed, Arjun found himself grappling not only with physical pain but also with the emotional toll of his confinement. The sounds of the rain outside his window, once a source of solace, now served as a cruel reminder of his own vulnerability. Trapped in his sick bed, he longed for the warmth of the sun and the freedom of movement that illness had stolen from him. But most of all today he was missing Diya.

Arjun sat alone in his dimly lit room, the soft glow of his phone screen illuminating the darkness around him. His thoughts swirled with a tumult of emotions, a tangled web of longing and apprehension. For months, he had tried to bury his feelings for Diya beneath the weight of his crumbling career, hoping to shield himself from the turmoil of emotional entanglement. But tonight, as the rain pattered against his window and the ache in his heart grew unbearable, he found himself unable to suppress the yearning that burned within him.

With a sigh, Arjun closed his eyes and whispered a silent prayer to the heavens above, a desperate plea born of his deepest desires. "Oh God, please make her call me," he murmured, his voice barely more than a whisper. "I need to hear her sweet voice, if only for a moment. It would lift my spirits like nothing else. Please…"

But just as quickly as the longing had surged within him, he pushed it away, chastising himself for his weakness, for daring to hope for something that seemed so out of reach.

And then, as if in response to his silent prayer, his phone rang, shattering the silence of the room with its shrill tone. Arjun's heart skipped a beat as he glanced at the caller ID, his eyes widening in disbelief. Could it be? Was it really her?

With trembling hands, he reached for his phone, his fingers hovering over the screen as he hesitated for a moment, his mind racing with a whirlwind of emotions. But in the end, curiosity and longing won out, and with a steadying breath, he swiped to answer the call.

"Diya?" he breathed, his voice barely above a whisper, disbelief coloring his tone.

The voice on the other end was soft and familiar, sending a shiver down Arjun's spine as he listened to her speak. It was her, his Diya, reaching out to him after all this time.

"Hey, Arjun, is everything alright?" she asked, concern lacing her words. "You sound… pale, weak."

Arjun hesitated for a moment, trying to brush it off. "Oh, it's nothing, just a bit tired," he replied, hoping to downplay any worries.

But Diya wasn't convinced. "No, something's not right. Tell me what's going on," she insisted, her tone firm yet gentle.

With a heavy sigh, Arjun finally relented. "I have malaria," he admitted quietly, his voice tinged with resignation.

Diya's heart sank at the news, her concern deepening. "Oh, Arjun, I'm so sorry to hear that," she murmured sympathetically. "You need to take care of yourself, especially when you're alone."

Arjun felt a rush of gratitude at Diya's caring words. "Thank you, Diya. It means a lot to hear you say that," he confessed, his voice soft with emotion.

Diya's voice was warm with reassurance as she offered practical advice. "Make sure you rest, drink plenty of fluids, and take your medication on time," she instructed.

Arjun couldn't help but smile at Diya's thoughtfulness. "Thank you, Diya. Just hearing your voice is enough to make me feel better," he admitted gratefully.

As they continued to talk, sharing stories and updates on their lives, Arjun felt a sense of comfort wash over him. Despite the distance between them and the challenges they faced, he knew that their connection remained strong.

"You know, Diya, things have been really rough for me lately. My career... it's not going anywhere. I feel like I'm stuck in a rut."

"I understand, Arjun. But you're not alone. I'm here for you. Tell me what's been going on."

"Well, ever since I joined ZCP, it's been one disappointment after another. My sales numbers are down, and I'm struggling to make any progress."

"I understand. But I know you. You're capable of so much more than you realize. But you lack focus. You must have it to accomplish what you want."

"Focus? But how do I find that when everything seems to be falling apart?"

"You find it by remembering your promise to me," Diya reminisced. "You told me you would become the best in what you do. And I believe in you, Arjun. You have the talent and the drive to succeed."

Arjun's eyes widened with sudden recollection, a wave of determination washing over him as he recalled the pledge he had made to her. At that moment, amidst his struggles, her words reignited a spark within him, reigniting his commitment to excel and fulfill his vow.

"You're right, Diya. I can't let myself be defeated by setbacks. I have to rise above them and become the best sales manager I can be."

"That's the spirit, Arjun. Believe in yourself, and nothing can stop you. I'll be rooting for you every step of the way."

"Thank you, Diya. Just hearing your encouragement has lifted my spirits. I won't let you down. I'll make you proud."

"I know you will, Arjun. Now go out there and show them what you're made of. I'll be cheering you on from afar."

"I will, Diya. And thank you, again, for always believing in me."

"Anytime, Arjun. Take good care of yourself. I will call you tomorrow again to check on your health."

As they bid each other goodbye, promising to keep in touch more regularly, Arjun couldn't help but feel a renewed sense of hope. For in Diya's caring words and genuine concern, he found solace in the midst of his illness, a reminder that even in the darkest times, there was still light to be found in the warmth of friendship.

15

March Forward

As Arjun returned to ZCP after his recovery, Charu approached him with concern.

"Hello, Sir, welcome back. How are you feeling?" she asked.

"Doing fine now. Just a bit of weakness," he responded.

Charu nodded with empathy. "I'm relieved to hear you're okay. If there's anything you need, just let me know," she offered warmly, displaying her support.

"I'm sure I will. If only you could assist me in making some progress in the business," Arjun remarked with a hint of frustration.

"Hmm, I'm not sure if this is good news or bad, but Mr. Brajesh came looking for you," Charu informed him.

"What? Why?" Arjun's tone was tinged with concern.

"He dropped by last Saturday. I'm not sure of the reason. I didn't dare to ask him," Charu admitted.

"He walked to the cubicle himself?" Arjun questioned.

"No, he drove in his SUV all the way from his cabin to his cubicle. What kind of question is that? Of course, he came by himself," Charu clarified.

"Oh dear! I'm in trouble. He might terminate my employment here," Arjun lamented, his worry palpable.

Charu raised an eyebrow, her expression incredulous. "He can't terminate you, Sir. You work for a different company altogether, and you don't report to him," she pointed out.

Arjun shook his head, a grim look crossing his face. "You don't understand, Charu. He has influence. He reports directly to the MD. He could squash me like a mosquito, and no one would even notice. Remember the day he gave me a piece of his mind over the phone? I am a dead duck," he explained, his voice filled with resignation.

"There's only one way to find out," Charu gave a supportive nod. He agreed, steeling himself for what lay ahead. "I'll go and knock on his door now and face him."

With a deep breath he made his way to Brajesh's office, ready to confront whatever awaited him head-on.

He tapped on the glass door of his office, signaling for permission to enter. As he entered the cabin, he noticed Brajesh seated behind his desk, his posture upright and commanding. The faint glow of the laptop screen illuminated his glasses, highlighting the intensity in his eyes as he focused on his work. Beside him, another figure occupied the sofa, their presence adding to the aura of authority that permeated the room. Brajesh exuded an air of confidence and control, his gaze piercing as it locked onto Arjun, silently assessing him as he stood at the threshold, feeling the weight of the moment settle upon him.

"Oh, Arjun, the insurance guy," Brajesh stated firmly.

"Yes, sir," Arjun stammered.

Upon hearing this, Brajesh dismissed the other person in the room with a few instructions, challenging him to succeed. Then, he wheeled his chair towards Arjun, who stood nervously, feeling Brajesh's gaze sizing him up.

"I heard you were unwell. What happened?" he inquired.

"Malaria, sir," Arjun replied.

"You appear frail. Are you not taking care of yourself?"

"It's due to the medication, sir. I'll recover soon."

"Alright. Before I address my main agenda for today, I want to emphasize that you should be more assertive and self-assured. In my office, anyone can knock and see me. You don't need appointments when you're just down the hall from my office. Is that clear?" Brajesh asserted.

"Yes, sir. Absolutely," Arjun responded.

Brajesh leaned back in his chair, his expression shifting from scrutiny to a hint of urgency. "My car insurance has expired for a month now. I need the new policy immediately," he declared, his tone decisive.

Without missing a beat, Arjun nodded, his professionalism kicking in. "I'll take care of that right away. Could I have your car papers, please?"

Brajesh wasted no time, immediately reaching for his phone and summoning his driver to fetch the necessary documents. As the papers arrived and Arjun began his assessment, Brajesh watched intently, his curiosity piqued by the process.

After a thorough examination and some calculations, Arjun presented him with a figure, causing Brajesh's eyebrows to raise in surprise. "25,768 rupees?" he echoed, clearly taken aback by the unexpectedly low amount for the premium payment..

Arjun, however, remained composed, explaining confidently, "Yes, sir. I managed to secure approval from our headquarters for a flat 20% discount on premiums for ZCP employees."

Brajesh's demeanor shifted, impressed by Arjun's strategic maneuvering. "That's very smart," he acknowledged, a hint of admiration coloring his voice as he recognized Arjun's resourcefulness and efficiency in securing such a beneficial deal. "But, just a discount of a few thousand rupees will not fetch you my business. Convince me on the offerings that you have", he said in a challenging tone.

"Certainly sir!"

As Arjun began to explain the various offerings of the insurance policy, Brajesh's attention seemed to wane, his focus drifting away. Sensing the need to re-engage him, Arjun racked his brain for a solution. Then, a light bulb moment struck him.

"Sir, I have a PowerPoint presentation detailing our car insurance policy features. Would you like me to share it with you via email?" Arjun suggested, hoping to reignite Brajesh's interest.

To Arjun's surprise, Brajesh didn't hesitate. Instead, he stood up abruptly, his demeanor suddenly energized. "No time for that. Let's head to the conference room. You can give me the presentation there," Brajesh declared, his tone decisive.

Caught off guard but unable to refuse, Arjun followed Brajesh to the conference room, feeling a mix of nerves and determination. As he began his presentation over a projector, he focused on delivering his points with clarity and conviction, knowing that this opportunity could make or break the deal.

Partway through Arjun's presentation, Brajesh interrupted him and made a call, summoning additional colleagues to the conference room. Soon, the room filled with executives in starched shirts and ties, all listening with keen interest. A rapid-fire Q&A session followed, where Arjun did his best to answer each question despite his limited knowledge in the insurance sector. He responded to everything to the best of his ability. After an hour, everyone left the conference room.

"How did it go, sir?" Arjun asked.

"You did really well, my boy! Just a piece of advice, though. If you don't know the answer to a question, just say so and promise to follow up. Never make up false information, which you were doing a bit too often. But I liked your confidence. These executives will need insurance in the near future and could be your potential clients. That's why I asked them to join and listen to you."

"Sir, I have a request. I would like our insurance services to be advertised in the monthly company email so that the entire ZCP staff is informed."

"Consider it done. Now, go ahead and make my day by delivering my car insurance."

"Absolutely, sir. Could you please ask your driver to take me to your car? Since your policy has expired, I need to take an impression of the chassis number as proof of inspection."

"Hmm. I see you are all alone! Don't you have any assistants for this task?"

"I do, sir. In fact, I have two."

"Then send them instead."

Taking a deep breath, Arjun explained the situation with Rajan and Ganesh.

"Is that so? Don't worry. Just wait and see."

Brajesh picked up his phone and called his assistant, instructing him to find both Rajan and Ganesh and bring them immediately. Shortly after, he was seen marching towards the cabin with Rajan and Ganesh in tow, who were walking nonchalantly.

As soon as Ganesh and Rajan entered the cabin, Brajesh's eyes blazed with fury. He launched into them with a voice that resonated ominously throughout the hall.

"Do you two have any idea how critical this is? Your behavior has been utterly disgraceful!" His voice was menacing, each word cutting like a knife. "How dare you neglect your responsibilities? This kind of incompetence is intolerable in this organization!"

Rajan and Ganesh stood frozen, their faces drained of color, looking as if they might collapse under the weight of his wrath. They were so terrified it seemed they might soil themselves.

Brajesh continued, his tone growing even darker. "You think you can shirk your duties and leave a professional like Arjun to do all the running around, picking up cheques and doing mundane stuff? He is new, and he's already demonstrated more dedication and competence than either of you. Your negligence is unacceptable!"

Arjun watched in stunned silence, his eyes wide as he took in the scene. He had never imagined witnessing such a fierce reprimand.

"If I hear one more complaint about either of you," Brajesh's voice dropped to a chilling whisper, "I will personally ensure you are thrown out of this campus without hesitation. From now on, you will follow Arjun's instructions precisely. Is that understood?"

Both Rajan and Ganesh nodded vigorously, too scared to speak.

"Good," Brajesh concluded with a final, icy glare. "Now get out from here and get things done for my insurance policy. Then join Arjun and do as he says."

Thereafter, Brajesh turned his gaze to Arjun, his expression softening slightly. "You don't worry now. Go ahead and get back to work," he instructed. "You won't have any more trouble from these two. They will run around the campus like rabbits."

Arjun nodded, feeling a mix of relief and determination.

"And remember," Brajesh continued, his tone now firm but supportive, "If you encounter any issues, don't hesitate to come to me. My door is always open for you."

With a final reassuring nod, Arjun left the room, feeling more confident and supported, ready to tackle his responsibilities head-on.

Delighted with how things had turned out, Arjun walked back to his cubicle, where he found Charu smiling knowingly.

"Did you hear what happened?" he asked, unable to hide his own grin.

Charu chuckled. "Oh, Sir. The entire hall did. The scolding Rajan and Ganesh got was so loud that everyone in the hall knows what went down."

Arjun shook his head in amazement. "I can't believe it. I never expected that kind of support from Mr. Brajesh."

In a short while, both Rajan and Ganesh arrived at Arjun's cubicle, carrying a bunch of papers in their hands. They approached Charu, who took the documents and immediately began working on the computer to generate Mr. Brajesh's policy.

Rajan and Ganesh then turned to face Arjun, their expressions filled with remorse. Their faces drooped with the weight of their apology.

"Sir," Rajan began, his voice earnest, "We're really sorry for how we've behaved."

Ganesh nodded in agreement. "We promise we'll work hard from now on and won't give you any more reasons to complain."

Arjun looked at them, seeing the sincerity in their eyes. "Alright," he said, his tone forgiving yet firm. "Let's make sure we all stay on top of our responsibilities from here on out."

With a mutual understanding established, they all turned their focus back to their tasks, ready to move forward with renewed dedication.

In the evening, Arjun headed to the Navi Mumbai office to report to Harish. Sitting in Harish's cabin, they recounted the day's events, sharing a laugh over the unexpected turn of events.

Arjun, still amazed, said, "When it was so easy to go to Brajesh and get things done, why didn't anyone else do it?"

Harish leaned back in his chair, smiling knowingly. "That's the bias of experienced people. They get intimidated by Brajesh's position and don't dare to approach him. You, being new, had no idea about his power in the company, so you approached him without much apprehension."

Arjun nodded, reflecting on this insight. "But it was risky, wasn't it?"

Harish's expression grew serious. "Absolutely. If Brajesh hadn't been supportive, he could have got you fired, the moment you called him for the first time. It was an unintentional gamble, but it paid off for you. Just be cautious and keep learning."

"Of course," said Arjun.

Harish leaned forward, his tone becoming more serious. "This doesn't mean that the business at ZCP will flourish on its own, Arjun. You have to keep working hard. If Brajesh took an entire presentation for one little insurance policy, you can imagine what the scheme of things to come will be like."

Arjun nodded, understanding the gravity of Harish's words. "I get it. This was just the beginning, right?"

"Exactly," Harish affirmed. "You'll need to be prepared, diligent, and consistently on top of your game. Brajesh is thorough and expects the best. But you've shown you can handle it. Keep that momentum going."

Harish's wisdom hit the nail on the head. Even with Rajan and Ganesh now playing by the rules and dancing to Arjun's tune, the business wasn't exactly skyrocketing. With the permission of Mr. Brajesh, daily emails were being bombarded to every ZCP employee. Despite the occasional deals for car and health insurance, the growth just didn't have that zing. Arjun couldn't help but notice that Rajan and Ganesh were more like errand boys than business generators. They excelled at fetching cheques and documents, but when it came to sparking new leads, they were about as effective as a wet firecracker.

Two months went by without Arjun making any significant progress. During this time, Harish summoned him and instructed him to go to the Dadar headquarters as Priya had requested his presence. Harish's tone was grave, hinting that Arjun might face a reprimand for his lack of progress.

Priya greeted Arjun with her characteristic suaveness, engaging in light conversation about his experiences in Mumbai over a cup of coffee. However, the tone shifted as Priya's demeanor turned serious.

"Arjun, we had great expectations from you regarding ZCP," she began, her voice now measured.

Arjun recalled the game she had played against him at the behest of Sharat and his heart raced, but he maintained his composure, hiding his emotions behind a neutral expression. He explained the challenges he faced with Ganesh and Rajan, detailing how he had navigated the situation and leveraged Brajesh's support.

Priya nodded. "I commend you for your resourcefulness, Arjun. However, in the corporate world, efforts alone don't suffice. What matters are results, which, unfortunately, you haven't delivered."

Arjun felt a knot form in his stomach as her words sank in. He knew what was coming next.

Priya gave him a subtle warning, her tone tinged with implications. "If you fail to perform, Arjun, we will have to consider taking steps. And there's only one direction for you to go in that scenario. I hope you understand that."

Arjun understood the gravity of the situation as he left Priya's office, the weight of her words hanging heavy on his shoulders.

Rishi, Saurabh, and Arjun gathered for drinks, their usual ritual to unwind and vent about the stresses of work. As they clinked their glasses, the conversation flowed naturally.

Rishi chuckled, raising his glass. "You know, even though I'm not exactly setting the world on fire at work, it's always you who gets the one-on-one sessions with Priya. What's a guy gotta do to get called into her cabin?"

Arjun rolled his eyes, smirking. "Well, at least neither of you has been warned about getting fired. That's something, right?"

Rishi raised an eyebrow, feigning jealousy. "Maybe I'll just start messing up on purpose so I can get some special attention from Priya too."

Arjun laughed, shaking his head. "Trust me, you don't want that kind of attention. But hey, cheers to surviving another week!"

They all laughed, easing some of the tension that had been building up.

Turning to Saurabh, Arjun asked, "So, Saurabh, what's the deal with that job offer from the other company you mentioned? Any updates?"

"Oh, it's happening soon, my friends." Then he leaned in with a mischievous grin. "Guess what, guys? There's going to be a big party next week to celebrate Zencorp Insurance's revenues crossing 1000 crores for the first time!"

Rishi raised an eyebrow in mock disbelief. "Wait, so even with both Arjun and I contributing absolutely nothing, the company still managed to hit that figure? Amazing!"

Arjun laughed, shaking his head. "How on earth do you know about this, Saurabh?"

Saurabh smirked. "Ah, the perks of being stationed at headquarters, my friends. You get all the juicy inside info. And guess what? There's going to be free, high-quality booze, and the who's who of the company will be there."

Rishi's eyes lit up. "Free booze? Now that's something to celebrate. Maybe I can get that audience with Priya at the party after all."

Arjun chuckled. "Just make sure you don't end up in her bad books like me. But hey, cheers to an upcoming night of pretending we actually contributed to that 1000 crores!"

Rishi leaned back with a mischievous glint in his eye. "You know what, guys? Maybe I'll just get drunk at the party and finally shed all my inhibitions. Who knows, I might even strike up a conversation with her!"

Saurabh chuckled, shaking his head. "Rishi, you're always head over heels for Priya. But tell me, who's the girl you keep talking to late at night on the phone?"

Arjun's eyebrows shot up in surprise. "Wait, what? You secretly talk to someone late at night?"

Saurabh nodded, a sly grin forming on his face. "Oh, yes. Rishi. I know it's a girl. Come on, spill the beans, Rishi. Who is she?"

After much teasing and pressure from Arjun and Saurabh, Rishi finally caved. "Fine, fine! It's Arpita from your department."

Saurabh's jaw dropped in disbelief. "Arpita? My deputy? Of all the girls in the city you found her?"

"Yes," Rishi announced with pride.

Saurabh shook his head in disbelief. "Rishi, what are you doing? That girl is an absolute nymphomaniac!"

Rishi shrugged, a devilish grin spreading across his face. "Exactly. That's the whole point. I'm setting her up to score! She is so ready to be in bed with me. I am just waiting for an opportune moment."

"God help you," Saurabh shrugged.

Arjun couldn't resist adding his own quip to the mix. "So, Saurabh, let me get this straight. She is your deputy, and it's Rishi who managed to score her?"

They burst into laughter once again, with Saurabh shaking his head in mock disbelief. "Hey now, let's not jump to conclusions! Besides, Rishi's always had a way with the ladies."

Rishi flashed a grin, raising his glass in mock salute. "What can I say? I'm just irresistible."

Their banter continued well into the night, each joke and jibe adding to the jovial atmosphere as they eagerly anticipated the upcoming party and the potential for even more outrageous antics.

16
Office Party

It was the party night, and the entire Mumbai team had gathered in a lavish banquet hall in Bandra. The venue was decorated with elegance and style, featuring shimmering chandeliers and luxurious drapes that added a touch of opulence to the celebration. The atmosphere was electric, with the blaring music setting a lively tone for the evening.

Booze was flowing freely from the well-stocked bar, where bartenders skillfully mixed drinks and served a variety of high-quality spirits. Colleagues mingled and laughed, their glasses clinking in a symphony of celebration. The dance floor was already packed with people letting loose, moving to the rhythm of the pulsating beats that filled the air.

Arjun, Rishi, and Saurabh were at the center of the action, enjoying the vibrant energy of the night. Rishi, true to his word, seemed more confident with every drink, his eyes scanning the room for Priya. Saurabh was cracking jokes, keeping the spirits high, while Arjun took it all in, savoring the break from the usual work stress.

Clusters of employees gathered in animated conversations, their voices rising above the music. The excitement was palpable as everyone celebrated Zencorp Insurance's milestone of crossing 1000 crores in revenue. The who's who of the company were in attendance, adding an extra layer of prestige to the event.

In one corner, a group was engrossed in a lively debate about the best sales strategies, while another cluster erupted in laughter over a shared joke. The open bar kept the drinks coming, and the servers moved gracefully through the crowd, offering trays of delicious hors d'oeuvres.

The DJ, sensing the high energy, switched to an even more upbeat track, and the dance floor's crowd responded with enthusiastic cheers and even wilder dance moves. The flashing lights and dynamic visuals added to the festive ambiance, making it a night to remember.

As the night went on, the three friends found themselves with fresh drinks, watching the dance floor's action. The music had taken on an infectious beat, and Priya was at the center of it, dancing with impressive and graceful moves. Her energy was captivating, and it was clear she was enjoying herself.

Rishi, unable to take his eyes off her, nudged Arjun and Saurabh. "Guys, look at Priya go. She's got some serious moves!"

Arjun chuckled, taking a sip of his drink. "No kidding. I think she missed her calling as a professional dancer."

Saurabh grinned, shaking his head in mock admiration. "Man, she's got more rhythm than a metronome. I'd probably trip over my own feet if I even try to match with her!"

Rishi, emboldened by the drinks, said, "Maybe I should go over there and join her. Show her some of my own moves."

Arjun raised an eyebrow, smirking. "Oh really? What moves are those, exactly? The two-left-feet shuffle?"

Saurabh laughed, clapping Rishi on the back. "Yeah, and don't forget the classic stumble-and-fall. Always a crowd-pleaser."

Rishi rolled his eyes but grinned. "Come on, guys. Have a little faith. Maybe she'll be impressed by my unique style."

As Priya danced, her eyes suddenly caught Arjun's. She flashed a huge smile and waved enthusiastically. Arjun, Rishi, and Saurabh exchanged confused glances, unsure of who she was waving at. Seeing him puzzled, she made her way towards them.

She stopped in front of Arjun, still radiating energy from the dance floor. "Arjun, you look too stressed. You need to relax and leave your work worries aside. That's what these parties are for—enjoying life!"

With a warm smile, she turned and danced her way back into the crowd.

Rishi was visibly deflated. "Great. Just great," he muttered, staring into his drink. "I try even to think about impressing her, and she ends up giving a pep talk to Arjun."

Saurabh, still grinning, teased, "Maybe she likes Arjun. Ever think of that? After all she has Sharat as her hubby! You know what he looks like!"

Rishi groaned, rolling his eyes. "Oh, fantastic. Just what I needed to hear." He sighed heavily and wandered off towards the bar.

Arjun watched him go, feeling a mix of amusement and sympathy. "Poor Rishi," he said to Saurabh. "He behaves like he wants to marry her?"

Saurabh shrugged, still smiling. "Well, it's the booze talking. But hey, I am sure it's all in good fun. He will be back to his senses as the booze gets down his head."

As the music blared and the party buzzed with excitement, Arjun spotted Sharat across the hall. He waved, trying to catch his attention, but Sharat merely frowned and turned away, deliberately ignoring him.

Before Arjun could ponder Sharat's cold reception, Devraj approached with a crooked smile. "Well, well, well, look who it is," Devraj began, his tone dripping with sarcasm. "Mr. Arjun, the star performer at ZCP."

Arjun narrowed his eyes, bracing himself for the inevitable jab. "What do you want, Devraj?"

Devraj chuckled, shaking his head. "Oh, just checking in. You know, you've been a complete failure at ZCP. No surprises there. Honestly, I thought you'd have taken my offer by now. I can still talk to Sharat and get you back under me. You might actually get somewhere with my guidance."

Arjun's jaw tightened, but he forced a calm response. "Thanks for the offer, Devraj, but I'm fine where I am. I don't need your help."

Devraj shrugged nonchalantly, his grin widening. "Suit yourself, Arjun. Just don't say I didn't warn you. This gig at ZCP isn't going to get any better for you. You might want to start looking for another job before it's too late."

Arjun's eyes flashed with determination. "I'll manage. Thanks for your concern."

Devraj gave a mocking salute and turned to leave, his laughter mixing with the party's noise. "Good luck, Arjun. You're going to need it."

His words and sarcastic smile had hit Arjun hard, leaving him feeling utterly defeated. He couldn't shake off the memory of Priya's stern warning about his performance and the looming threat of a pink slip. The weight of his failures pressed down on him, and he felt devastated.

Saurabh noticed his friend's distress and tried to calm him down. "Hey, Arjun, don't let that jerk get to you. You'll figure things out."

But Arjun was spiraling, his thoughts dark and chaotic. He grabbed another drink, then another, each one dulling his senses further. The alcohol numbed his pain, but it also clouded his judgment. He reached for a cigarette, something he hadn't done in years, and muttered to himself, "I need a matchbox."

As he stumbled through the crowded banquet hall, he lost sight of Saurabh and wandered aimlessly, unable to distinguish faces or places. The vibrant party around him blurred into a confusing haze of lights and sounds.

"Does anyone have a matchbox?" he called out, his voice slurring. His desperation turned into a mantra as he repeated, "I need a matchbox, I need a matchbox."

Finally, he saw an older man standing in a dimly lit corner, smoking a cigar. Arjun staggered over and blurted out, "Do you have a matchbox, dude?"

The older man looked at him with a bemused expression but struck a match and held it out. Arjun leaned in, the flame flickering in the dark, and lit his cigarette.

"Thanks, buddy," he mumbled, his words barely coherent. "You're a good friend."

He took a deep drag, but immediately started coughing violently, the smoke burning his throat and lungs. The room spun around him, and his legs gave way, sending him crashing to the floor.

The next thing Arjun remembered was Saurabh's strong arms dragging him towards a corner. He could barely keep his eyes open, the world a swirling mess of colors and sounds.

"Come on, Arjun," Saurabh said urgently, his voice cutting through the fog. "Let's get you out of here."

Arjun managed a weak, lopsided smile, still clutching his cigarette, now half-burned.

As Saurabh dragged him away from the chaos of the party, Arjun's mind drifted in and out of consciousness, the night's events becoming a distant blur. The last thing he saw before everything went black was Saurabh's determined face, guiding him through the darkness.

As Saurabh guided Arjun to a quiet corner where fresh air circulated, he gently poured water on Arjun's face, coaxing him back to his senses. Arjun jolted awake, blinking rapidly as the cool water shocked him into awareness.

Once Arjun seemed more lucid, Saurabh leaned in, his expression grave. "Do you know what you did out there? You asked for a matchbox from none other than the MD of Zencorp himself."

Arjun's eyes widened in disbelief, the fog of intoxication momentarily clearing. The weight of Saurabh's words hit him like a ton of bricks, sending a chill down his spine. Even in his drunken state, he understood the gravity of his actions.

A stunned silence hung between them as Arjun struggled to comprehend the magnitude of what he had done. The revelation was like a lightning bolt, illuminating the severity of his recklessness. He felt a wave of embarrassment and panic wash over him, realizing the implications of his audacity.

The realization left Arjun speechless, his mind reeling with the implications of his impulsive behavior. He glanced around the room, suddenly acutely aware of the watchful eyes and murmured whispers surrounding him.

With a sinking feeling in his chest, Arjun turned to Saurabh, his voice barely above a whisper. "Take me home, Saurabh. Please."

Saurabh nodded, concern etched on his face. "Of course, Arjun. But first, I need to find Rishi. I can't seem to locate him."

Arjun sighed, feeling a pang of guilt for dragging Saurabh into his mess. "He must be fine. I am not feeling well. Let's just focus on getting out of here."

Together, they navigated through the crowded hall, Arjun leaning heavily on Saurabh for support. As they made their way towards the exit, Arjun couldn't shake the sinking feeling in his chest, knowing that his impulsive actions had only deepened the hole he was in.

As they reached home, Saurabh carefully guided Arjun to his bed, gently laying him down as he drifted into a deep slumber. Arjun's snores filled the room, a testament to the exhaustion and intoxication that had overtaken him.

After ensuring Arjun was comfortable and safe, Saurabh quietly tiptoed past Rishi's room. The door was bolted from the inside, and the steady hum of the ceiling fan echoed softly through the hallway. Saurabh breathed a sigh of relief, knowing that Rishi had returned home before them and had already retired for the night.

With a sense of reassurance, Saurabh made his way to his own room, feeling the weight of the evening's events finally beginning to lift from his shoulders. He slipped under the covers, the warmth of his bed enveloping him as he succumbed to the embrace of sleep.

As Saurabh emerged from his room the next morning, his thoughts still foggy from sleep, he made his way down the hallway toward Rishi's room. However, as he turned the corner, he collided with someone, causing him to stumble back in surprise.

Standing before him was a girl, clad in nothing but a towel. Recognition flashed across Saurabh's face as he exclaimed, "Arpita!"

Arpita, her cheeks flushing crimson with embarrassment, hastily tried to tighten the towel around her, stammering out apologies. "Oh my god, sir, I'm so sorry! I didn't know you were Rishi's flatmate..."

Saurabh waved off her apologies with an embarrassing gesture, though his own cheeks were tinged with a faint blush. "It's alright, Arpita. Just do me a favor and get dressed, okay?"

Arpita nodded fervently, still flustered, and scurried off to Rishi's room to change.

Shell-shocked by the unexpected encounter, Saurabh made his way to the kitchen, his mind racing with a mixture of amusement and disbelief. As he began to prepare his morning coffee, Arpita reappeared, now fully dressed but still visibly embarrassed.

Saurabh couldn't help but tease her gently. "Well, Arpita, I hope you won't be asking for a leave today after that little mishap."

Arpita's cheeks flushed even darker as she mumbled another apology and hastily made her way out of the front door, eager to escape the awkwardness of the situation.

Saurabh watched her go with a chuckle, shaking his head in amusement. It was certainly an unexpected start to the day, but he couldn't deny that it had added a touch of humor to an otherwise ordinary morning.

As Arjun groggily awoke, his head pounding from the excesses of the previous night, he muttered, "I have such a headache."

Saurabh, ever the attentive friend, handed him a steaming cup of coffee. "Here, drink this. It might help."

Arjun nodded gratefully, taking a sip of the coffee and wincing at the bitter taste. As he slowly began to feel more alert, Saurabh couldn't resist sharing some news to lighten the mood.

"Oh, by the way, our friend Rishi had quite the night last night," Saurabh began, a mischievous twinkle in his eye. He then proceeded to recount the unexpected encounter with Arpita in the hallway, causing Arjun's eyebrows to shoot up in surprise.

"Arpita? In just a towel? Oh, that's embarrassing," Arjun exclaimed, his headache momentarily forgotten in his amusement.

Saurabh nodded, his lips quirking into a grin. "You have no idea. But don't worry, she's fine now. Just a little flustered."

As Rishi strolled into the room with a victorious grin plastered across his face, Arjun and Saurabh couldn't help but exchange amused glances.

"Well, well, well, look who's here," Saurabh teased, gesturing towards Rishi. "The man of the hour!"

Rishi chuckled, his grin widening. "Oh, you have no idea, my friends. Last night was legendary!"

Arjun raised an eyebrow, curiosity piqued. "Legendary, you say? Do tell."

And so, with a dramatic flourish, Rishi launched into a colorful retelling of his escapades from the previous evening – from charming Arpita at the party to bringing her home and, well, sealing the deal.

Saurabh whistled appreciatively, while Arjun shook his head in mock disapproval. "Ah, Rishi, you sly dog. But next time you plan on doing stuff with her, go someplace else.

It's very awkward to have my deputy running around, half naked in my home."

"Sure dude!"

"And what about Priya? I'm sure she'll be heartbroken!" Saurabh teased.

Rishi shrugged nonchalantly. "Who cares? I am having fun with Arpita!"

However, the jovial mood took a turn when Arjun's own misadventures from the party were brought up.

"And then, get this," Saurabh began, unable to contain his amusement, "Arjun here asked none other than the MD of Zencorp for a matchbox! And he obliged him by lighting his cigarette himself!"

"Shit! It was him," Arjun's face turned crimson with embarrassment as Rishi burst into uproarious laughter. "No way! You actually did that, Arjun?"

Arjun sheepishly nodded, feeling the weight of his foolishness settle upon him. "Yeah, I did. It was a moment of, uh, impaired judgment."

The trio dissolved into fits of laughter, the absurdity of the situation impossible to ignore. Despite the embarrassment, Arjun couldn't help but join in, realizing that sometimes, the most humiliating moments could also be the most hilarious.

"So I guess this is it! My termination letter must have been sent through an email!"

"Oh come on! He is the MD of a company that has thousands of employees. He would have forgotten this by now," said Rishi.

"That's wishful thinking!"

As Arjun finished his coffee and the details of the morning's events sunk in, he couldn't help but chuckle at the absurdity of it all. Despite the headache and the lingering embarrassment from the night before, there was a sense of camaraderie and laughter in the air, reminding him that even amidst the chaos of life, these were moments of levity and friendship to be cherished.

125

<h1 style="text-align:center">17
Let the Sales Begin</h1>

As Arjun stared at the quarterly performance report, his heart sank. His name was at the bottom, while Devraj's was proudly at the top. The weight of his dismal performance was heavy on his mind when his phone buzzed with an incoming call from Devraj. Reluctantly, he picked it up.

"Hey there, Arjun!" Devraj's voice oozed with smugness. "Saw the report, huh? Quite the performance gap between us, don't you think?"

Arjun gritted his teeth, trying to keep his composure. "Yeah, Devraj, I saw."

Devraj continued, not missing a beat. "You know, it's just a matter of time before I clinch that Top Sales Manager title for the third time in a row. And do you know what that means? A Promotion to Branch Manager is almost guaranteed."

Arjun's heart raced. "Branch Manager, huh? Good for you."

"Not just any branch, my friend," Devraj said, his tone dripping with superiority. "Harish's moving up to Regional Manager, and the Navi Mumbai branch will need someone capable. Guess who's likely to be in charge there? Yours truly."

Arjun's stomach churned. The thought of Devraj becoming his boss was almost unbearable. "So, you'll be my boss then?"

"Looks like it," Devraj replied, chuckling. "Imagine that. I can finally whip that branch into shape. Maybe give you some tips on how to actually sell."

Arjun forced a laugh, though it sounded hollow even to his own ears. "Yeah, sure. Tips from the best."

Devraj's tone turned slightly more serious, but still condescending. "Seriously, Arjun, you need to step up your game. Maybe one day you can reach my level. Until then, keep trying."

"Thanks for the advice," Arjun managed to say, though every word felt like a struggle.

"Alright, enough of the pep talk," Devraj said, clearly pleased with himself. "Just wanted to give you a heads-up. Prepare yourself for the new boss."

As the call ended, Arjun sat there, the reality of his situation sinking in. The fear of Devraj becoming his boss loomed large, but deep down, a flicker of determination ignited. He couldn't let Devraj win so easily. It was time to fight back and reclaim his position.

As Arjun went about his daily routine, he found himself deep in conversation with Charu, Rajan and Ganesh about the stagnant business. They were seated in the small meeting room, the faint hum of office activity serving as a backdrop to their discussion.

"I'm really concerned about our numbers," Arjun began, his tone filled with frustration. "We've been sending out the daily emailers and trying to engage with potential clients, but the business just isn't taking off."

Charu nodded, her expression thoughtful. "I know, Arjun. We've been pushing hard, but it seems like we're missing something. Maybe we need to rethink our approach."

Rajan, sitting across the table, chimed in hesitantly, "Maybe we should focus more on personal outreach? Like, visit potential clients directly?"

Ganesh nodded in agreement, adding, "And maybe offer some limited-time promotions or incentives to attract more interest?"

Arjun sighed, running a hand through his hair. "Those are good ideas, but we need to be strategic about it. We can't afford to waste resources on efforts that won't yield results."

Charu leaned forward, her voice calm and steady. "I think we need to analyze our current client interactions and identify where we're falling short. Maybe there's a particular aspect of our service that needs improvement."

Arjun nodded, appreciating her insight. "You're right, Charu. Let's gather some data on our client interactions and see if we can spot any patterns. Rajan, Ganesh, I want you two to help with this analysis. Let's brainstorm ways we can better meet our clients' needs and stand out from the competition."

Rajan and Ganesh exchanged glances, their expressions showing a mix of determination and uncertainty. "We'll do our best, boss," Rajan said, trying to sound confident. "Tell us what we should do?"

"It's time to be proactive. You need to start making cold calls and talking to clients directly."

Rajan and Ganesh exchanged uneasy glances. "But we're not trained for this," Ganesh protested, his voice wavering.

Arjun waved off their concerns. "You don't need formal training to strike up a conversation. Just be friendly and professional. Here," he said, pushing the landline phone towards them, "Here, give it a try."

As Rajan hesitantly picked up the phone again, his hands were slightly trembling. He dialed another random number from their client list, his face a mixture of determination and dread. The phone rang a few times before someone answered.

"Hello?" came a gruff voice from the other end.

"Uh, h-hello, this is, uh, Rajan from, uh, Zencorp Insurance," Rajan stammered, his voice cracking. "How… how are you today?"

There was a brief pause before the person responded, sounding slightly confused, "I'm fine. Who is this again?"

Rajan gulped. "Uh, Rajan… from Zencorp Insurance. I, um, wanted to talk to you about some, uh, exciting new insurance offers we have. Do you, uh, have a moment to, um, discuss?"

The person on the other end sighed. "I guess. What are these offers?"

Rajan fumbled with his notes, the paper rustling loudly near the receiver. "Well, uh, we have, um, car insurance and, um, health insurance. They're, uh, really great and, uh, could save you… money?"

The person sounded increasingly impatient. "What kind of savings are we talking about here?"

Rajan blinked rapidly, clearly flustered. "Oh, um, a lot! Like, uh, you know, 20% off if you're, um, an employee of, uh, ZCP."

There was a long silence. "I'm not an employee of ZCP."

Rajan's eyes widened. "Oh! Uh, right. Well, uh, maybe you know someone who is? Or, um, maybe you have a car?

Or, um, you like saving money?"

The person on the other end chuckled, more amused than interested. "You're really not good at this, are you?"

Rajan turned a shade of crimson, looking over at Arjun for help. Arjun mouthed, "Stay calm."

"Uh, no, I'm... new. But, um, I'm trying! So, uh, how about it? Want to hear more?"

The person sighed again. "You know what? Sure, kid. Let's hear your pitch."

Rajan glanced at Arjun, who gave him an encouraging thumbs-up. With a deep breath, Rajan continued, stumbling over his words but managing to convey the main points. By the end of the call, the person had agreed to a follow-up, albeit more out of pity than interest.

When Rajan hung up, he slumped back in his chair, a mixture of relief and embarrassment on his face. Ganesh burst out laughing, and even Arjun couldn't suppress a grin.

"Well, that was... something," Arjun said, patting Rajan on the back. "But hey, you got through it. Next time, just try to be a little more confident."

Rajan managed a weak smile. "I'll try, boss. But man, that was nerve-wracking!"

Ganesh, still chuckling, picked up the phone. "Alright, boss. Why don't you show us how to do it."

Arjun took over the receiver and demonstrated. "Watch this." Dialing another number, he waited for an answer. "Good morning, this is Arjun from ZCP Insurance. I hope I'm not catching you at a bad time. We have some exciting new insurance plans that could really benefit you. Do you have a moment to discuss how we can help you save money?"

The person on the other end responded positively, and Arjun smoothly continued the conversation, showcasing the key points of their offers and engaging the client with ease. After a few minutes, he ended the call with a satisfied smile.

"See? It's all about being confident and making the client feel like they're getting something valuable," Arjun explained. "Now, you try."

Ganesh picked up the phone, dialing with confidence. When the call connected, he echoed Arjun's approach, "Good morning, this is Ganesh from ZCP Insurance. Am I speaking to Mr. Sharma? I hope I'm not interrupting. We have some excellent new insurance plans that I think you'll find very beneficial. Do you have a moment to chat?"

As the conversation progressed, Ganesh managed to keep the client engaged, even scheduling a follow-up call to discuss further details. When he hung up, he looked over at Arjun, who nodded approvingly.

"That's more like it. Great job, Ganesh. Rajan, you're up next. Just keep it conversational and remember, you're offering something that can really help them."

With each subsequent call, Rajan and Ganesh grew more confident, their initial apprehension giving way to a sense of accomplishment. Sometimes even Charu joined them and made calls in her spare time. They focused their energy as they continued their cold-calling efforts, guided by Arjun's encouraging words and practical tips.

After a couple of days of making cold calls, Rajan and Ganesh approached Arjun with a mix of excitement and urgency. They gathered around Arjun's desk, their faces serious but their eyes sparkling with new ideas.

"Boss," Rajan began, his voice steady but intense. "We've been analyzing our approach, and we think we've identified what's missing."

Arjun looked up, curiosity piqued. "Alright, tell me."

Ganesh leaned forward, his tone earnest. "We need three key elements to really make an impact: a standout insurance product, a utility bundle, and an event to create buzz."

Arjun's interest was clearly piqued. "Go on."

Rajan continued, "First, we need an insurance product that stands out. Something unique with clear, compelling benefits that make it an easy choice for clients."

Arjun nodded, leaning back thoughtfully. "That makes sense. And the second thing?"

Ganesh took over, "We need to bundle the insurance with something useful. Like a complimentary health check-up with health insurance or a car maintenance package with car insurance. This added value will make our offers irresistible."

Arjun's eyes brightened for a moment, then he shook his head slightly. "Car maintenance and health check-up bundles are offered by every other company. We need something truly unique."

Rajan frowned, thinking hard. "Something unique... What if we offered personalized financial planning sessions with every policy? Or maybe access to exclusive lifestyle experiences, like travel discounts or wellness retreats?"

Ganesh's eyes lit up. "Or how about a concierge service that helps with day-to-day tasks? People value time and convenience."

Arjun's expression shifted from thoughtful to inspired. "Now we're talking. These ideas have the potential to set us apart. What's the third piece?"

Rajan grinned, "We need to create a buzz. An event or campaign that captures attention and gets people talking. Maybe a financial planning seminar or a community health fair. Something big that draws people in and gives us a platform to showcase our products."

Just then, Charu, who had been listening from her desk, interjected with a brilliant idea. "What if we organized a month-long event and tied up with an authorized vendor to provide free Pollution Under Control (PUC) certificates on campus? People could get their pollution checks done conveniently, and we could promote it as an event where we collect insurance data from the clients."

Arjun's eyes widened with excitement. "That's a fantastic idea, Charu! It offers a real service to people, something they need and can use. And it gives us the perfect opportunity to engage with potential clients in a meaningful way."

Rajan and Ganesh exchanged impressed glances, nodding in agreement.

Charu continued, "You know, the executives here value time over money. To get their PUC done, they have to wait in long queues because there are very few authentic PUC vendors at petrol pumps. If we offer this free service right here on campus, they'll surely appreciate it. It's convenient and saves them a lot of hassle."

Arjun nodded, energized. "That's a great point, Charu. Convenience is key. If we can save them time and provide a valuable service, they'll be more likely to engage with us for their insurance needs."

Ganesh added, "Plus, it shows we're considerate of their time and needs. That can build a lot of goodwill."

Rajan chimed in, "And while they're here for the PUC, we can talk to them about our insurance products and the unique bundles we're offering. It's the perfect opportunity."

Arjun stood up, inspired. "Alright, let's do this and plan this event around the PUC certificates. Great job, everyone!"

Rajan and Ganesh exchanged proud smiles. "Thanks, boss," Rajan said.

Harish came through with a reliable PUC vendor, thanks to his connections. With Brajesh's assistance, they secured permission and space for the event. Extensive email advertising ensured that the executives on campus were well aware of the opportunity. As anticipated, they flocked to the venue for their PUCs. Meanwhile, Rajan and Ganesh diligently collected data on the expiry dates of their car insurance policies.

The sight of an insurance service right in their backyard surprised many attendees. Through this event, numerous leads were generated. Arjun, Rajan, and Ganesh found themselves inundated with calls from potential clients, while Charu worked tirelessly to process insurance policies. The sales graph skyrocketed, reaching a point of self-sustainability.

Now, anyone in need of insurance knew exactly where to go: that bustling cubicle where Arjun, Rajan, Ganesh, and Charu operated tirelessly. Their teamwork and dedication had turned the tide, making ZCP the go-to destination for insurance needs on campus. For over two months, Arjun heard nothing from Priya about the warning. He took this as a sign that his position was now secure.

Just when everything seemed to be going smoothly for Arjun, the tides abruptly turned. One morning, Harish approached him with a grim expression.

"Arjun, we have a bit of a problem," Harish said, sighing heavily. "The company is facing some litigation, and the court has barred us from selling any new policies. We're not allowed to go out in the field and do new business."

Arjun's jaw dropped. "Are you serious? Just when things were finally picking up!"

Later that day, Arjun met up with Rishi and Saurabh, hoping for a bit of comic relief amidst the chaos.

Rishi, always quick with a quip, chuckled. "So, Arjun, what's the plan now? Selling insurance policies in the black market?"

Saurabh laughed, patting Arjun on the back. "Maybe we should set up a secret insurance speakeasy. Password: Premiums."

Arjun couldn't help but laugh at the absurdity of the situation. "Honestly, guys, what am I supposed to do? We were finally gaining momentum, and now this!"

Saurabh leaned in with a grin. "Look at the bright side, Arjun. At least we won't have to deal with angry clients for a while."

Rishi nodded. "Yeah, no more frantic calls about claims or expired policies. We could use the downtime to, I don't know, master the art of knitting sweaters in the office?"

Arjun groaned, shaking his head. "Very funny, Rishi. But seriously, what are we sales people supposed to do all day?"

Rishi laughed. "I was so bored, I decided to explore the local train system to kill time. I took four round trips to their final destinations and counted the number of stations."

Saurabh raised an eyebrow. "Seriously? Four round trips?"

Rishi replied with a grin. "I even made up a game where I'd predict how many people would get on and off at each stop. Spoiler: I was almost always wrong."

Arjun chuckled. "You must've looked like a total weirdo to the other passengers."

"Oh, definitely," Rishi said, nodding. "At one point, this kid asked if I was a train inspector. I told him, 'No, I'm just an insurance guy with nothing to insure."

Saurabh burst out laughing. "That's classic, Rishi. Next time, take notes and write a guidebook: 'The Bored Office Worker's Guide to Mumbai's Local Trains."

As they continued to banter, Arjun couldn't resist throwing in another teasing remark. "What about Arpita? Why don't you pass the time with her instead?" he said with a grin.

Rishi shook his head, chuckling. "I'm not a Hercules, man. I can't go on with her for 8 hours a day."

They all burst into laughter, the absurdity of the situation lightening the mood.

"But seriously," Rishi continued, his tone shifting. "The girl is getting weirder by the day. I actually want to get rid of her."

Saurabh raised an eyebrow. "I thought you were enjoying the... attention."

Rishi sighed. "At first, maybe. But now, it's just too much. She's constantly calling and texting, and it's getting out of hand. I have to agree with you, Saurabh—she's a damn nymphomaniac."

Arjun chuckled, shaking his head. "Well, at least your love life isn't boring. But yeah, maybe it's time to have a chat with her."

Rishi nodded. "Definitely. I need to set some boundaries before I completely lose my mind."

Saurabh smirked. "Who would've thought our Rishi, the office Casanova, would be overwhelmed by too much attention?"

Now the conversation shifted. Arjun leaned back, a heavy sigh escaping his lips. "It's like I was finally gaining some traction, and now this."

Saurabh nodded sympathetically, swirling his drink. "Yeah, it's a setback, no doubt. But hey, guess what? The company has a Top Sales Manager of the year award. One for each of the top performer in each vertical."

Arjun's interest piqued. "Yes. Devraj was talking about it today. He flaunted that he has won it two times in a row. What about it?"

Saurabh leaned in, a glimmer of excitement in his eyes. "Well, why not aim for that? It's a chance to show what you're made of and get recognized for it."

Arjun's expression shifted, determination replacing frustration. "You know what? You're right. I'm going to aim for that award."

"Rishi, you should also try for that," Saurabh asked Rishi.

"Nah! I am least bothered about being known as an winner of some trashy insurance sales award! I have no interest in it. You see, I want to enjoy life and do only as much is needed. I deliberately keep my sales figures good enough to keep my boss happy and low enough so I can stay happy. If you exceed your targets they will keep increasing it. So I don't take that much pain."

Saurabh grinned, raising his glass. "So it's Arjun then! Let's drink to Arjun, the future Sales Manager of the Year!"

They clinked their glasses together, the sound echoing in the room. Later, as Arjun sat alone with his thoughts, he whispered to himself, "I'll win that award... and then I'll call Diya to let her know I've kept my promise."

18

The Audit

One evening, as Arjun handed his sales report to Harish, he noticed a round cylindrical object on the desk. "What's that?" he asked.

Harish grinned, picking it up. "This? It's a stencil for making pencil impressions. We use it to insure vehicles whose policies have expired. No need for a physical inspection—just a little office magic."

Arjun's eyes widened. "Isn't that illegal?"

Harish laughed. "Technically, yes. But it's how we get business. Everyone does it. Think of it as a shortcut."

Arjun frowned. "Harish, this feels risky."

Harish leaned back. "Relax, Arjun. We only use it when the client is desperate and we need to close the deal fast. Teach Veer and Ganesh too, but use it wisely."

Arjun sighed. "I don't know, Harish. This feels off."

Harish patted his shoulder. "Trust me, buddy. It's all part of the game. You're smart—you'll figure it out."

Arjun left, shaking his head. "Great, now I'm part of the pencil mafia," he muttered, half-amused, half-worried.

One day, during a routine audit, the auditors were meticulously skimming through the documents at the office. The atmosphere was tense and quiet, everyone hyper-aware of the scrutiny.

In the midst of this, Ganesh, completely oblivious to the auditors' presence, sauntered into the cubicle with a hefty stack of papers. He whistled a cheerful tune, plopped the papers down, and pulled out his trusty stencil.

Without a second thought, Ganesh began making pencil impressions, diligently tracing away. The auditors, initially focused on their work, started to notice the rhythmic scratching sound. They looked up, puzzled, and exchanged bewildered glances.

One of the auditors, Mr. Mehta, cleared his throat loudly. Ganesh, still oblivious, continued his task, even humming a bit louder. Another auditor, Ms. Sharma, couldn't contain her curiosity. She leaned over and stared directly at Ganesh, her eyebrows raised.

Finally, Arjun, seeing the impending disaster, rushed over, his face a mix of panic and forced calm. "Ganesh, what are you doing?" he hissed, eyes darting towards the auditors.

Ganesh looked up, surprised. "Oh, hey, boss! Just making some quick impressions here. What's up?"

Arjun's eyes widened in horror. "In front of... them?" He pointed subtly towards the auditors, who were now fully attentive and slightly amused.

Ganesh followed Arjun's gesture and finally noticed the auditors. His face turned pale. "Oh... uh, these impressions... are, uh... purely for demonstration purposes," he stammered, trying to stuff the stencil back into his bag nonchalantly.

Mr. Mehta couldn't help but chuckle. "Interesting demonstration, Mr. Ganesh. Very... educational."

Ms. Sharma nodded, her lips twitching into a smile. "Indeed. Maybe you could give us a full tutorial later."

Arjun intervened quickly, "Thank you, Mr. Mehta, Ms. Sharma. We'll make sure Ganesh saves his demonstrations for after hours."

Ganesh, now beet-red, nodded vigorously. "Yes, yes, of course. So sorry about that."

As the auditors turned back to their work, still chuckling, Arjun glared at Ganesh. "Next time, look around before you start your 'demonstrations,' alright?"

Ganesh nodded sheepishly, whispering, "Got it. No more stencils during audits."

Arjun sighed, shaking his head as he walked away, thinking, "This job never ceases to surprise me."

19

The MD and his Porsche

As Arjun entered his cubicle he found Charu in a state of urgency, frantically trying to call someone. As soon as she saw her she asked him to immediately head to Brajesh's office. Arjun's curiosity piqued as Charu relayed the urgent summons from Brajesh. With a furrowed brow, he pondered the significance of such a sudden and anxious request. "What could it be about?" he mused aloud, the uncertainty evident in his voice.

Charu shrugged helplessly, her expression mirroring Arjun's bewilderment. "I'm not sure," she admitted, her tone tinged with concern. "But he sounded quite anxious. Better not keep him waiting."

Taking a deep breath to steel himself, Arjun squared his shoulders and made his way to Brajesh's cabin. With each step, his mind raced with possibilities, the urgency of the situation weighing heavily on him.

As he entered the cabin, Arjun found Brajesh pacing back and forth, his usual air of confidence replaced by an uncharacteristic restlessness. "You wanted to see me, sir?" Arjun ventured, his voice laced with apprehension.

Brajesh paused in his tracks, his gaze locking onto Arjun with intensity. "Yes, Arjun," he replied, his tone grave. "I've received some troubling news, and I need your expertise to help navigate through it."

The gravity of the situation hit Arjun like a ton of bricks, his mind racing to anticipate the nature of the problem. "What's happened?" he asked, his voice tinged with concern.

Brajesh hesitated for a moment before revealing the details, his words laden with urgency. He leaned in, his voice low and urgent, Arjun felt a shiver run down his spine. "Arjun, we've got a problem," he began, his words punctuated by the gravity of the situation. "The big boss, our MD, has imported a brand new Porsche. It's his pride and joy, but it's currently stranded at the port."

Arjun's eyes widened in disbelief. "Why?" he interjected, his mind racing to comprehend the severity of the situation.

Brajesh shook his head, a grim expression etched on his face. "It's missing one crucial detail: insurance," he revealed, his tone tinged with urgency. "Somehow, someone overlooked the need to insure it. And now, unless I can secure insurance before the boss arrives this evening, there's going to be hell to pay."

A surge of adrenaline coursed through Arjun as the reality of the situation sunk in. "We can't let that happen," he declared, his voice firm with determination. "I'll move mountains to get that insurance sorted, whatever it takes."

Brajesh nodded, a glimmer of hope flickering in his eyes. "I knew I could count on you, Arjun," he said, his voice tinged with gratitude. "But remember, time is of the essence. The boss expects his porsche in his garage by today evening. It is his beloved Porsche."

With a sense of urgency propelling him forward, Arjun wasted no time springing into action. Every second counted as he raced against the clock, his mind focused on the daunting task ahead. Failure was not an option—not when the reputation of the company and the wrath of the MD hung in the balance.

Arjun's heart sank as Brajesh laid out the stark reality before him. "So, what are we supposed to do?" he asked, his voice tinged with frustration and anxiety.

Brajesh sighed, his expression grave. "We'll need to draft a legal document—a document that meets the standards required by international customs," he explained, his tone heavy with the weight of the task at hand. "This isn't something that Charu can simply type up on her computer."

Arjun's mind raced as he absorbed Brajesh's words, grappling with the weight of the responsibility thrust upon him. "But how?" he wondered aloud, his voice tinged with uncertainty.

Brajesh's expression softened, understanding Arjun's dilemma. "I know it's a lot to take in, Arjun," he conceded, his tone sympathetic. "But we have no choice. We need those insurance papers and we need it now! You need to figure out something fast."

Arjun nodded, determination flickering in his eyes. "I'll do it," he declared, his voice firm with resolve. "I'll make sure everything is in order."

As he left Brajesh's office, Arjun's mind buzzed with a million thoughts, each one more urgent than the last. How would he navigate this labyrinthine maze of bureaucracy and logistics? He didn't have all the answers, but one thing was certain: failure was not an option.

Returning to his cubicle, Arjun took a deep breath, steeling himself for the challenges that lay ahead. With a sense of purpose driving him forward, he began to formulate a plan—a plan to overcome the seemingly insurmountable obstacles and emerge victorious in the face of adversity.

As Arjun's mind raced with the weight of the situation, he turned to Charu, his trusted colleague, and poured out the details of the daunting task ahead. Charu's expression mirrored his own sense of overwhelm as she absorbed the gravity of the situation. "This is beyond me, Sir," she admitted, her voice tinged with uncertainty.

With the clock ticking relentlessly, Arjun wracked his brain for a solution. And then, like a bolt of lightning, a thought struck him: Saurabh, his friend, the underwriter. Who better than him to consult. With a sense of urgency, he reached for his phone and dialed Saurabh's number, his fingers trembling with anticipation.

Arjun's heart soared with relief as Saurabh's words washed over him like a beacon of hope. "A cover note?" he repeated, his voice tinged with a mixture of astonishment and gratitude.

Saurabh nodded, his expression calm and assured. "Yes, a cover note," he confirmed, his tone brimming with confidence. "It's a temporary document that holds legal validity for a period of sixty days. Harish should have it in his possession. All you need to do is have him sign and stamp it, and we'll have an authentic insurance document ready to go."

Arjun felt a surge of optimism course through him as he realized that there was indeed a solution to their dilemma. "That sounds perfect," he exclaimed, his voice infused with newfound energy. "I"ll get in touch with Harish right away and get this sorted out."

As the call to Harish connected, he wasted no time in explaining the gravity of the situation, his words tumbling out in a frantic rush.

"Harish, it's Arjun," he began, his voice tinged with urgency. "We have a major problem with the MD's Porsche. It needs insurance documents urgently, or there will be hell to pay."

There was a brief pause on the other end of the line before Harish responded, his tone skeptical. "You're joking, right?" he said incredulously, disbelief evident in his voice.

Arjun's heart sank at Harish's initial reaction, but he knew there was no time to waste in convincing him of the seriousness of the situation. "I wish I was," he replied earnestly, his voice tinged with desperation. "But this is as real as it gets. Can you get your hands on the cover note as soon as possible?"

"Right away! Tell me the details of the car like registration and chassis number."

As Arjun relayed the details of the car to Harish, his heart pounded with anticipation, every second ticking by like an eternity. With each passing moment, the weight of the situation bore down on him like a crushing weight, the urgency of the matter palpable in the air. Brajesh could call him any moment for the document.

Harish's voice crackled through the phone, his words a lifeline in the darkness of uncertainty. "I have the cover note signed and ready here," he said, his tone urgent. "Now I need the premium amount to finalize it."

With trembling hands, Arjun punched the numbers into the calculator, his breath catching in his throat as he awaited the result. But as the figures appeared on the screen, his heart sank like a stone.

The premium amount loomed before him like a lavish spectacle, the digits mocking him with their magnitude. Frantically, he performed the calculation again, but the result remained unchanged, a reminder of the enormity of the task at hand.

Turning to Charu for help, Arjun watched as she inputted the data into the software, her fingers flying across the keyboard in a blur of motion. But even as she worked, the outcome remained the same, the numbers refusing to budge from their staggering sum.

With each passing moment, the tension in the room reached a fever pitch, the weight of the situation bearing down on them like an unyielding force. And as Arjun relayed the figures to Harish, even he was left dumbfounded by the astronomical amount.

"Shit, that's the price of my brand new car!" Harish exclaimed, his disbelief echoing through the phone like a thunderclap.

There was no time for further contemplation, no room for hesitation. With a sense of grim determination, Harish swiftly inscribed the amount onto the cover note, his hand steady despite the turmoil raging within.

"I'm sending it over to ZCP right away," he declared, his voice resolute. And with that, the wheels of fate were set in motion, as the fate of the MD's Porsche hung in the balance, its future teetering on the brink of uncertainty.

As the office peon darted into the cubicle with the cover note in hand, Arjun couldn't help but crack a joke to alleviate the tension that hung thick in the air.

"Did Harish send you in a Porsche?" he quipped, a wry smile tugging at the corners of his lips. "You're here faster than lightning!"

The peon chuckled nervously, clearly feeling the weight of the situation despite Arjun's attempt at levity. But there was no time for further banter, no room for anything but swift action.

Taking the cover note from the peon, Arjun raced to deliver it to Brajesh, each step feeling like an eternity as he made his way through the bustling office.

And as he finally handed over the document, a sense of relief washed over him, the weight of the moment lifting from his shoulders like a burden lifted.

Brajesh's eyes widened in disbelief as Arjun placed the document in his hands. For a moment, he was speechless, his gaze fixed on the cover note as if trying to decipher its significance.

"You did it," he finally murmured, his tone a mixture of astonishment and relief. "I didn't think it was possible."

Arjun couldn't help but feel a surge of pride at Brajesh's reaction. Despite the odds stacked against them, they had managed to pull through in the eleventh hour.

"It wasn't easy," Arjun admitted, his voice tinged with exhaustion. "But we made it happen."

Brajesh nodded, a faint smile playing at the corners of his lips. "Well, consider this a job well done, Arjun. You've certainly earned your stripes today. Now come with me. I will show you what a brand new Porsche looks like!"

As Arjun sat next to Brajesh in his car, they arrived at the port trust warehouse where the Porsche was being held. Arjun was captivated by the car's grandeur. The plush leather seats offered comfort, the dashboard boasted cutting-edge technology, and the potent engine emitted a distinct energy.Upon reaching the warehouse, Arjun's amazement only grew as he laid eyes on the Porsche. It stood proudly in the sunlight, radiating luxury and sophistication. Arjun couldn't look away, mesmerized by its sleek design and flawless craftsmanship.

In awe, Arjun found himself admiring the luxury vehicle. It was his first time being so close to such a high-end car, leaving him completely entranced. For a moment, he forgot about the chaos and urgency of the situation, lost in the beauty of the moment. It was a surreal experience, one that Arjun knew he would never forget. And as they set about resolving the issue with the customs department, Arjun couldn't help but feel a newfound appreciation for the power of determination and resourcefulness.

"The problem is sorted, and it's all thanks to you, my boy," Brajesh praised. "You've done well. Here's the thing: the Big Boss brings in a new car every quarter. From now on, they'll all be insured by you! My assistant will reach out to you beforehand to take care of it."

With a nod of gratitude, Arjun stepped back, allowing Brajesh to inspect the document at his leisure. As he watched him pore over the details, he couldn't shake the feeling that they had just narrowly averted a disaster of epic proportions. But for now, at least, the crisis had been averted, and all that remained was the sweet relief of victory.

As the adrenaline rush of the moment began to subside, Arjun's mind raced with a new realization. The premium amount for just one imported car, as staggering as it was, surpassed his fortnightly target by a landslide. It was a sobering thought, one that brought into sharp focus the magnitude of the task they had just accomplished.

But amidst the whirlwind of emotions, Arjun couldn't help but feel a glimmer of hope. This successful resolution could be the catalyst he needed to propel himself closer to his ultimate goal: becoming the best sales manager in his vertical.

Brajesh grinned at Arjun, his eyes twinkling with excitement. "Hey, I'm headed to the MD's bungalow to deliver the Porsche. He's eager to see it. Want to come along?"

Arjun's curiosity was piqued. "You mean in the Porsche, sir!"

"Yes!"

"Sure, why not?"

The MD's driver expertly maneuvered the Porsche out of the port. As Arjun settled into the passenger seat, he was immediately awestruck by the car's luxurious interior. The leather seats were buttery soft, cradling him in a cocoon of comfort. The dashboard was a marvel of modern engineering, with sleek lines and a futuristic design. Every surface was meticulously crafted, from the polished wood accents to the brushed aluminum details. The ambient lighting cast a soothing glow, enhancing the feeling of opulence. It felt more like stepping into a 3 BHK luxury flat than a car, with all the amenities one could dream of seamlessly integrated into the space.

As they cruised through the city, the powerful engine purred beneath them, a reminder of the sheer power and sophistication of the machine. Arjun couldn't help but admire the state-of-the-art technology embedded throughout the interior – the advanced infotainment system, the climate control that adjusted to their preferences, and the sound system that made even the hum of the engine seem like a symphony.

After a short drive, they arrived at the MD's bungalow. The grandeur of the place was immediately evident. The bungalow stood tall and majestic, its white walls gleaming in the sunlight. The sprawling lawn was meticulously manicured, with perfectly trimmed hedges and vibrant flowerbeds adding bursts of color. A grand fountain stood in the center of the driveway, water cascading down in a mesmerizing display.

The entrance was nothing short of palatial. Massive double doors, adorned with intricate carvings, welcomed them. As they stepped inside, the opulence continued. The marble floors gleamed, reflecting the light from the crystal chandeliers overhead. The high ceilings were adorned with elegant moldings, and the walls were lined with artwork that spoke of both taste and wealth. Expansive windows offered stunning views of the lush gardens outside, creating a seamless blend of indoor and outdoor luxury.

Arjun was in awe of the sheer magnificence of the place. It was a far cry from the hustle and bustle of his usual surroundings, and he couldn't help but feel a sense of wonder at the life the MD led. As he followed Brajesh and the driver, he marveled at the opulence and grandeur that seemed to define every corner of the bungalow.

As the driver expertly parked the Porsche inside the grand garage, both Brajesh and Arjun sighed and admired the luxurious vehicle. As Arjun stepped out of the Porsche, his eyes fell on the MD standing just outside the garage. The MD was a tall, distinguished-looking man in his early fifties, with a commanding presence that immediately drew attention. His silver hair was neatly combed back, and he wore a crisp, tailored suit that spoke of his impeccable taste. His eyes were sharp and assessing, yet there was a warmth in his smile that put Arjun slightly at ease. He exuded an air of confidence and authority, clearly a man used to being in charge and making decisions. Arjun could feel the weight of the MD's gaze as he approached, his heart pounding with a mix of fear and excitement.

They were immediately met by the MD, whose eyes sparkled with excitement as he approached his prized possession. His enthusiasm was palpable, and Arjun felt a twinge of anxiety as he remembered the incident at the office party when he had naively asked the MD for a matchstick. He could only imagine what the MD might do if he recognized him.

The MD beamed at Brajesh, shaking his hand firmly. "Job well done, Brajesh. I can't thank you enough for bringing my new toy home so swiftly."

Brajesh, always eager to share credit, smiled and gestured towards Arjun. "It was all due to Arjun's efforts, sir. He's the one who made sure everything went smoothly."

Arjun hesitated for a moment but then stepped forward hastily. The MD's eyes narrowed as he scrutinized Arjun, trying to place his face. "Who is this kid?" he asked, curiosity evident in his voice. "I swear I remember you from somewhere."

Suddenly, recognition dawned on the MD's face. He pointed at Arjun and exclaimed, "Wait a minute, you're the one who asked me for a matchbox at the office party!"

Arjun's face flushed with embarrassment, his heart pounding in his chest. He was certain he was in for a scolding or, worse, some form of professional reprimand. But to his surprise, the MD's stern expression melted into a wide grin, and he burst into laughter.

"Of all the nerve!" the MD guffawed, clutching his sides as he laughed heartily. "Asking the MD for a matchbox! You've got guts, kid. I like that!"

Arjun's tension eased slightly, though he still felt a bit sheepish. The MD's laughter was infectious, and soon even Brajesh was chuckling. Arjun managed a small, awkward smile, relieved that the situation hadn't turned sour.

The MD clapped Arjun on the shoulder. "Don't be embarrassed, son. It's good to see some boldness around here. Now, let's get this beauty inside and celebrate."

As they moved inside the palatial bungalow, Arjun couldn't help but feel a mixture of relief and newfound confidence. The MD's unexpected reaction had transformed a potentially humiliating moment into one of camaraderie and light-heartedness.

The MD escorted Brajesh and Arjun into his expansive, immaculate lawn. The lush greenery stretched out in front of them like a perfectly manicured carpet. Ornamental trees and vibrant flowers bordered the area, creating a serene, picturesque setting. A sophisticated stone pathway led them to a shaded seating area with elegant outdoor furniture. The air was filled with the subtle fragrance of blooming jasmine and the gentle sound of a nearby fountain added to the tranquil atmosphere.

As they settled into the plush chairs, the well-groomed housekeeping staff member approached with a gleaming silver kettle of tea. With practiced precision, he poured the steaming tea into exquisite silverware cups and offered them to the guests. Arjun accepted his cup, feeling the warmth seep into his fingers as he took a careful sip.

The MD turned to Arjun with a welcoming smile. "So, Arjun, tell me about yourself. Where do you come from?"

Arjun, still somewhat awestruck, recounted his background. "I come from Delhi, sir. I joined Zencorp right after graduation. It's been quite a learning experience so far."

Arjun then briefly told him his experience at Zencorp so far, avoiding the bitter ones though.

The MD nodded, his eyes twinkling with interest. "I remember my early days too. You know, I started as a door-to-door salesman. Those were challenging times, but they taught me resilience and the importance of understanding my customers. That's how I built Zencorp from the ground up."

Arjun listened intently. "That's inspiring, sir. It must have taken a lot of determination."

"It did," the MD agreed. "But more than that, it was about learning from every failure and not being afraid to take risks. Tell me, Arjun, what do you find most challenging about your work?"

Arjun thought for a moment. "I'd say it's meeting targets while maintaining customer satisfaction. Balancing the two can be tough."

The MD leaned back, sipping his tea. "That's a common challenge in sales. Always remember, customers are your biggest asset. Understand their needs, and the targets will follow. Have you ever had a customer interaction that taught you something significant?"

Arjun smiled, recalling an incident. "I received a panicked call from a health insurance customer late in the evening. He was at the hospital trying to get his sick father admitted, and the staff were giving him the runaround. They were asking for documents he didn't have and were not willing to process the cashless admission. I could hear the desperation in his voice, so I decided to help personally."

The MD's eyes widened slightly. "That's impressive, going above and beyond like that."

Arjun smiled modestly. "Thank you, sir. I called the hospital and met with the customer. I spoke directly with the hospital administration, explained the situation, and provided them with the necessary documentation from our side. I stayed there until the admission was successfully processed and his father was settled in the ward."

The MD nodded appreciatively. "That's commendable, Arjun. It shows dedication and empathy. How did the customer react?"

Arjun chuckled softly, recalling the moment. "He was immensely grateful. He told me that without my help, he wouldn't have known what to do. Later, he sent a heartfelt thank-you email to our office, praising our service. It felt good to make a real difference in someone's life."

The MD leaned back, clearly impressed. "That's the kind of dedication that makes a difference, Arjun. In this business, it's crucial to remember that behind every policy is a person with real needs and emotions. Your actions exemplify the values we strive to uphold at Zencorp."

Arjun felt a surge of pride at the MD's words. "Thank you, sir. It was a learning experience for me as well. It reinforced the importance of empathy and going the extra mile for our customers."

The MD smiled warmly. "Stories like these reassure me that the future of Zencorp is in good hands with young professionals like you. Always keep that spirit alive, Arjun. It's what sets us apart."

Arjun nodded, feeling more determined than ever. "I will, sir. Thank you for your encouragement."

The MD's eyes lit up. "Arjun! People in sales and marketing often underestimate the power of empathy. It's not just about closing deals; it's about building relationships. I admire the energy and drive of fresh graduates like you. They are not corrupted by the pressures of business targets expectations of superiors. There's so much potential there, and I believe in nurturing it. Always stay curious and never stop learning."The MD sipped his tea thoughtfully, then set his cup down on the table. "Arjun, with your dedication and drive, I wouldn't be surprised if you have some big aspirations here at Zencorp."

Arjun nodded, a determined look in his eyes. "Yes, sir, I do. One of my main goals is to win the Top Salesman of the Year award. I've been working towards it ever since I joined."

The MD raised an eyebrow, a hint of a smile playing on his lips. "That's an ambitious goal, considering you are a fresher. What drives you to aim for that?"

Arjun took a deep breath. "It's not just about the recognition, sir. It's about proving to myself that I can excel in this field. I want to show that with hard work and dedication, I can achieve great things. Plus, I believe that winning this award will open up more opportunities for me to grow within the company. Perhaps that should be enough gratification for me."

The MD nodded approvingly. "That's a great mindset, Arjun. Ambition is important, but so is the journey you take to get there."

As the MD looked at his watch, he stood up and excused himself. "I have another meeting now, but it was a pleasure talking to you, Arjun. Keep pushing forward."

Arjun nodded in admiration as the MD briskly moved away from him. But then he stopped midway and thought of something. He turned towards Arjun and looked at him with a thoughtful expression. "Take it as a challenge, Arjun, nothing else. Don't lose sleep over it. Who knows, this might be the last time we meet, but if you win that award, I'll send you a congratulatory email with every staff in Zencorp in the CC. This should be enough gratification for you and the best that I can do for you for bringing home my Porsche."

Arjun was overwhelmed with emotions. He felt a surge of determination. "Thank you, sir. That means a lot. I'll do my best."

The MD smiled warmly. "I'm sure you will. Just remember, success is not just about hard work but also about working smart and staying true to your values." The MD then trodded away disappearing almost like a genie.

For Arjun, the entire experience felt surreal. Meeting the MD in person, traveling in a Porsche, and receiving such valuable advice—it was a day he would never forget. As they drove away, he couldn't help but feel a sense of excitement for what lay ahead, fueled by the encouragement and wisdom he had gained.

20
No good Deed Goes Unpunished

Charu approached Arjun with a worried expression. "Sir, I've made a serious mistake with the data entry in the software."

Arjun looked up, concerned. "What happened?"

Charu took a deep breath. "I accidentally attributed the premium for one of your policies to another agent's code."

"Can you even do that?" Arjun asked, bewildered.

"Unfortunately, yes," Charu admitted. "Since the software is online and centralized, I have access to the list of all agents within the Mumbai region. Today, I accidentally clicked on someone else's code."

Arjun sighed, running a hand through his hair. "Great, just what I needed. Can you show me how this happened?"

Charu nodded and led him to the computer, navigating through the portal step by step. She opened the list of all agent codes attributed to different sales managers.

As they scrolled through the list, Arjun's eyes widened when he saw where the mistake had landed. "You've got to be kidding me," he muttered under his breath. Charu had accidentally attributed his business to none other than Devraj's code.

Frowning, Arjun couldn't help but make a sarcastic comment, "Of all people, it had to be Devraj. Just my luck."

Arjun asked her, "Can you reverse it?"

Charu shook her head, looking genuinely apologetic. "Once the data entry is made and the money is credited to the account of the agent associated with that sales manager, nothing can be done. Especially since it's month-end, no changes are allowed in the software."

Arjun sighed in frustration, muttering to himself, "Of course, just when things were going well." He ran a hand through his hair, trying to think of a solution. "So, there's absolutely no way to fix this?"

Charu looked sympathetic but firm. "I'm really sorry, Sir. The system locks everything down at the end of the month. We'll have to report it, but it will not reflect into your revenue."

As Arjun was cursing his luck, his phone rang. It was Devraj.

"Hey, Arjun! Thanks for the favor, buddy," Devraj's voice dripped with mockery. "I see you've decided to gift me some business at the month-end. How generous of you!"

Arjun clenched his jaw, trying to stay calm. "It was a mistake, Devraj. Don't read too much into it."

"Oh, sure, sure," Devraj continued, chuckling. "Reminds me of your early days when instead of selling, you ended up buying your customer's own policy. Ah, the memories!"

"Alright, Devraj. You've had your fun. Now can we move on?"

"Not so fast," Devraj said, his tone turning smug. "You should really forget about that Best Sales Manager award. My numbers are already better than yours, and with Sharat backing me, it's practically mine. Better luck next year!"

Arjun gripped his phone tightly, trying not to let Devraj's words get to him. "We'll see about that, Devraj. Enjoy your moment."

"Oh, I will," Devraj said, laughing before hanging up.

Arjun stared at his phone, the call disconnected, feeling a mix of anger and determination.

"Charu, please be careful next time," Arjun frowned.

"I am very sorry sir. Won't happen again," said an embarrassed Charu.

Arjun took a deep breath and turned to her. "We need to figure out exactly how this mistake happened. Can you walk me through it again?"

Charu sighed, "The account numbers associated with the agent codes are almost identical. I got confused and clicked on the wrong one."

"Show me those account numbers," Arjun demanded.

Charu opened the portal, revealing the nearly indistinguishable numbers. Arjun leaned in, his eyes narrowing as he studied the screen. He took over the mouse from Charu, scrolling through the data with intense focus. The silence in the room grew heavy with anticipation. Then suddenly Arjun's eyes widened.

"Charu!"

"Sir?"

"These accounts numbers are not similar, but they are the same! Every digit! That is why you got confused and committed this mistake."

"What??"

"Yes! All these account numbers belong to the same person! Means there is a single person associated with a different agent code!"

"I..I don't understand sir," Charu gave a bewildered look.

Minutes ticked by, each second heightening the tension. Then, suddenly, a wicked smile spread across Arjun's face. "I've got you Devraj, I've got you by your balls now," he muttered under his breath. He turned to Charu, his eyes gleaming with excitement. "You, Charu, are a genius! Your mistake is a eureka moment for me."

Charu looked bewildered. "What do you mean? What did you find?"

Arjun chuckled darkly, "I'll explain everything later. For now, just know that you've unintentionally handed me a golden opportunity. Thank you, Charu."

Charu's confusion deepened as she watched Arjun walk away, a cryptic smile playing on his lips. The atmosphere buzzed with the intensity of his revelation. She shook her head, still in the dark but sensing that Arjun had transformed their blunder into a deadly advantage. A thrill of anticipation coursed through her as she pondered what he had uncovered and how it would alter their fates.

Arjun pulled out his phone and dialed a familiar number. "Hi, Saurabh. I need your help with something!"

21

Loose Conections

One night, both Saurabh and Rishi arrived home late, together. As Saurabh unlocked the door, he couldn't help but notice a scooty parked right in front of it. He wondered whom it belonged to, as it had never been seen there before.

As they made their way into the hallway, they were startled by a loud feminine scream. The next thing they saw was a girl darting around the hall, clad in nothing but a towel.

Saurabh couldn't believe his eyes. "Arpita?? Not again," he muttered to himself, recognizing her instantly. Arpita looked at him, her eyes wide with panic.

"Sorry, sir!" she stammered, clutching her towel desperately.

Before Saurabh could even process what was happening, another girl burst into the hall, her face twisted in fury. She lunged at Arpita, who squealed and scrambled to avoid her.

Rishi, just stepping outside from his room, saw the chaos unfolding and gestured wildly at Saurabh. "Saurabh, stop her!"

Saurabh, reacting on instinct, grabbed the angry girl just in time. "Whoa, whoa, hold on!" he said, struggling to keep her from launching herself at Arpita.

The girl flailed, trying to break free. "Let me go! She deserves this!"

Meanwhile, Arpita was hopping around, trying to secure her slipping towel, looking like a frantic, oversized chicken.

Arjun hurried over, stepping between the two girls. "Everyone, calm down! What is going on here?"

The furious girl glared at Arpita. "She... she...!"

Arpita, still wrestling with her towel, squeaked, "It's not what it looks like!"

Saurabh, holding the angry girl back, shot a bewildered look at Rishi. "Care to explain?"

Rishi, finally persuaded enough and with both girls calmed down, took a deep breath and introduced the new girl. "Guys she is Devyani, my girlfriend!" Saurabh and Arjun were left utterly shocked. Rishi had never mentioned her before, and they were taken aback by the sudden revelation. They both looked at each other and then towards Devyani. Confusion painted their faces as they glanced between Rishi and Devyani. She stood there, a stunning vision, with an air of fierce determination that could rival an angry goddess. Saurabh couldn't help but feel a pang of guilt for ever doubting Rishi's taste in women. Devyani was undeniably attractive, and it left them wondering why Rishi would ever consider cheating on her.

Saurabh couldn't contain himself. "Wait, wait, wait. You mean to say, you've got this stunning goddess right here, and you've been messing around with Arpita?"

Arjun chimed in, equally incredulous. "Seriously, Rishi? Why in the world would you cheat on her?"

Rishi, looking a bit sheepish, tried to explain. "Guys, it's not what you think. Arpita and I, well, it's complicated."

Devyani, arms crossed and a fierce glint in her eye, shot them a glare. "Complicated my foot! You've got some explaining to do, Rishi."

As Devyani's tirade escalated, her accusations cutting through the air like daggers, Saurabh intervened, urging Arpita to retreat to privacy and gather herself.

"Arpita, could you please grace us with your fully clothed presence?"

Arpita, flustered: "Um, yes, of course, Sir!" She scuttled off to her room, towel still wrapped around her, leaving a trail of apologies in her wake. As Arpita dashed off to cover up her modesty, Rishi and Devyani reluctantly followed Arjun's lead, their expressions a mix of confusion and exasperation. Saurabh and Arjun exchanged amused glances, fully aware that they were wading into the absurdity of the situation.

Arpita reappeared fully clothed after a few minutes and disappeared from the house in a dash.

"Rishi, Devyani, it's better you guys sort this thing out in private," said Arjun.

Reluctantly, Devyani followed Arjun's lead, her anger simmering beneath the surface as she and Rishi retreated to the confines of his room. Saurabh and Arjun exchanged a glance, silently hoping that the couple would find common ground and mend their fractured relationship.

What ensued was a marathon of tears, wails and tantrums, with Devyani venting her frustrations and Rishi trying to salvage the situation. Arjun and Saurabh found themselves unwitting audience to the late-night drama, unable to interject as the verbal fireworks unfolded. Long after midnight, they heard the door creak open, signaling Devyani's departure. The sound of her scooter fading into the distance marked the end of the tumultuous evening.

Resigned to addressing the fallout in the light of day, Arjun and Saurabh retreated to their beds, hoping for a more peaceful tomorrow.

The next morning, Arjun and Saurabh gathered in the kitchen, bleary-eyed and nursing cups of strong coffee. The events of the previous night were still fresh in their minds, and they couldn't help but discuss the spectacle they had witnessed.

Saurabh took a sip of his coffee and sighed. "Well, that was something. I don't think I've ever seen such a dramatic exit."

Arjun chuckled, shaking his head. "Yeah, Devyani really gave Rishi a piece of her mind. He deserved it. I thought she was going to dismantle the whole room at one point."

Saurabh nodded, looking serious. "I wonder how Rishi's holding up. Should we check on him?"

At that moment, Rishi walked into the kitchen, looking like he hadn't slept a wink. His hair was disheveled, and dark circles ringed his eyes. He poured himself a cup of coffee and slumped into a chair.

"Morning," he muttered, clearly exhausted.

"Morning," Arjun and Saurabh echoed, exchanging glances.

Arjun broke the silence first. "So, Rishi, what happened after Devyani left? Are you okay?"

Rishi sighed deeply. "Not really. She was furious. I tried to explain, but she wasn't having any of it. She stormed out, and I doubt she's going to talk to me anytime soon."

Saurabh leaned forward, a hint of concern in his voice. "Why didn't you tell us about Devyani before? And what were you thinking with Arpita?"

Rishi ran a hand through his hair, clearly stressed. "I don't know, man. I messed up, big time. Devyani's amazing, and I don't know why I got involved with Arpita. I guess I was just being stupid."

Arjun gave a sympathetic nod. "We all make mistakes, Rishi. But you've got to figure out how to make things right, if you still can. But honestly, if I were her, I will never absolve you of the crime you have committed."

Rishi took a deep breath. "I'm going to try and reach out to Devyani today, see if she'll listen. As for Arpita, that was definitely a mistake. I need to sort my life out."

Saurabh clapped him on the shoulder. "Good luck, buddy. And remember, we're here if you need anything."

Rishi managed a small smile. "Thanks, guys. I appreciate it. But honestly, I think I've lost both of them. Devyani's probably done with me, and Arpita...well, she seemed pretty pissed off too. I've really screwed up."

The three friends sat in silence for a moment, sipping their coffee and reflecting on the chaotic night before. It was clear that Rishi had a lot of work to do to mend his relationships, but at least he had Arjun and Saurabh by his side, ready to support him.

Breaking the silence with a mischievous grin, Arjun quipped, "Don't worry, Rishi, you still have Priya."

Saurabh burst into laughter, and even Rishi couldn't help but chuckle despite his predicament. "Yeah, right. With my luck, she'll probably end up yelling at me too."

The light-hearted moment lifted their spirits slightly, reminding them that, no matter what happened, they had each other to lean on.

22
The Tide Turns

❦

It was the morning of the final quarter's end. The finance and operations teams had worked tirelessly to complete the accounts and balance sheets. Today would reveal who had clinched the title of best sales manager and who had generated the highest business. Devraj, exuding confidence, arrived at the office with a smile and a cup of coffee in hand. He sat down and eagerly opened his laptop, repeatedly refreshing his email, waiting for the anticipated message from the finance department that would unveil the sales manager rankings.

Finally, the email arrived. Devraj's heart raced with anticipation as he opened it with a confident smile. As expected, he was the top sales manager with the highest business contribution in the entire Mumbai region. He punched the air in excitement, feeling victorious.

But then, another email popped up with a subject line that read, "Top Sales Manager Award." Devraj opened it eagerly, his excitement mounting. However, his expression quickly turned to disbelief. His name was nowhere on the list of top sales managers. The award had gone to someone else entirely. He frantically scrolled through the email, his heart sinking with each passing second. His name was absent from the entire list. He read the email repeatedly, his hands trembling, but each time, his name was missing. Devastation washed over him, and he felt a lump in his throat. Shocked to the point of tears, Devraj's triumphant morning had turned into a nightmare.

"How could this be?" Devraj thought, panic rising within him. "When I am clearly the top business generator, why haven't I received the award? And what about my promotion?" These questions raced through his mind as he tried to make sense of the situation. Desperate for answers, he called his boss, Sharat, but there was no response. He dialed frantically, but Sharat didn't pick up. Devraj felt a wave of nausea wash over him.

Just then, another email popped up on his screen. This one was from the Head Office. He opened it with trembling hands and read:

"You are hereby summoned to the Head Office immediately to discuss a grave matter. Leave all current work with immediate effect and do not engage in any business activities until further notice."

Devraj's heart sank. There was no mistaking the implication—suspension. His world seemed to crumble around him as the weight of the situation hit him like a ton of bricks. Moments ago, he had been eagerly anticipating the award for himself. Now, it felt like he was plummeting off a cliff. He closed his laptop, took a deep breath, and headed towards the Head Office.

***

Rishi, Saurabh, and Arjun sat on their rooftop, enjoying their customary weekend drinks. The sun was setting, casting a warm glow over the city. The atmosphere was relaxed, but there was an undercurrent of excitement.

"So, Rishi, Saurabh," Arjun leaned back, a drink in his hand, "describe it for me. I want every detail vividly."

Saurabh took a sip of his drink, leaning forward with a grin. "Alright, Arjun. It was a spectacle, let me tell you."

Rishi chimed in, "It all started when Devraj walked into the Head Office, looking like he was going to vomit."

Saurabh continued, "Right. He was pale, sweating bullets. The moment he stepped into the office, you could feel the tension. Everyone knew something big was about to go down."

Arjun nodded, urging them to go on. "And then what happened?"

Saurabh leaned closer, lowering his voice for dramatic effect. "He was called into the conference room. There was our Regional Head, Mr. Desai, and other bunch of bigwigs from the Head Office there, including Sharat. They were waiting for him, looking like they were ready to pounce."

Rishi added, "Devraj was barely holding it together. When he spoke he sounded like he was constipated. He kept glancing around, probably hoping for some miracle to save him. But there was no escape."

Saurabh chuckled, "Yeah, and then Sharat laid into him. He started listing all the discrepancies they had found. The fake insurance agents, the commissions being siphoned off into Devraj's account. It was brutal."

"But then it was Sharat himself who encouraged him. He did it all at his behest didn't he?", enquired Arjun.

"Yes and although Devraj did try to bring in his name, but he had no proof. All the money trail led to Devraj and he had no way to prove that he had transferred that money to Sharat."

"Must have been cash dealings! So how did they find out? Was it really all because of that mistake by Charu?", Rishi said.

Arjun nodded, "Yeah, it all happened when Charu accidentally attributed my business to Devraj's code? That mistake made me dig deeper into the software and I scanned all those agent codes. I found that Devraj had created a bunch of fake agents, all funneling commissions to bank accounts belonging to him."

Saurabh smirked, "And you, being the genius you are, reported it to me. And I by the virtue of being an underwriter, recognized the issue and flagged it to the higher-ups with all the paper trail and evidence. That was the beginning of the end for Devraj."

Saurabh continued, "So, back at the Head Office, Mr. Desai was relentless. He went through every detail, every fake agent. Devraj tried to deny it at first, but the evidence was overwhelming. I could hear Mr. Desai screaming that he should thank him for not handing him to the police for financial fraud."

Rishi added, "When they finally asked for his resignation, you could see the defeat in his eyes. He knew it was over."

Arjun took a sip of his drink, savoring the moment. "And to think, just a while ago, he was so confident about winning the award and getting promoted. He had even anticipated becoming my boss and making my life hell!"

Saurabh nodded, "It was poetic justice. He had been cheating the system for so long, and it finally caught up with him."

"Why do you think Mr. Desai didn't go for prosecution?", Arjun asked.

"That would have been in the news then and the company's reputation would have suffered. Besides an investigation might have brought in Sharat's name in to the picture."

Rishi raised his glass, "Well he messed with the wrong bunch of musketeers, didn't he?"

"Yeah sure! So now what happens to Sharat?", Asked Arjun.

"There was no evidence against him. But once Devraj went away, he was called by Mr. Desai separately. He was reprimanded for his actions. His promotion has been denied. He would stay as the Branch Manager."

"That's nasty! But he could still get back at you Arjun. You should be careful.", Said Rishi.

"No he won't. Harish has been promoted as Regional Manager now and Sharat will have to report to him.", Saurabh revealed.

"That's great!", Rishi said.

They all clinked their glasses, laughing and enjoying the moment. Arjun felt a sense of accomplishment. It wasn't just about bringing down Devraj; it was about standing up for what was right. And in that moment, surrounded by friends and the glow of the setting sun, he knew he was on the right path.

Next day Arjun arrived at the Navi Mumbai office to see the entire office well decorated and all his colleagues standing up for him. Harish was standing in the front and as soon Arjun entered, he gave him a tight hug.

"I am so proud of you! Congratulations Arjun!", Said Harish

"It should be me who should be congratulating you for becoming our Regional Manager. Congratulations Harish! But did you mean to congratulate me for this Devraj episode?"

"Thanks. I can understand. Due to the climax of your real life underdog movie you must have missed this entirely."

"Missed what?", Arjun asked in heavy anticipation.

"Devraj was the top Sales Manager in the entire Mumbai region. In his absence the person ranked next to him won that award. However there are the best Salesman awards vertical wise. And guess who has generated the highest business in your vertical?"

"Who?"

"Check your mail and see for yourself!"

Arjun opened up his laptop and checked that mail from with Subject Best Sales Manager awards. It was his name in the category of his vertical.

"Dear God! How did I miss that?"

"Everyone except you, knows about it! This is because the MD himself wrote a mail, congratulating you, with the entire Zencorp staff in CC."

Arjun went back to the day when he had met the MD. "As promised," he thought to himself.

"You are the first ever fresher in the history of Zencorp to do it! Every fresher will be inspired by you. We will sing praises of you in front of any freshers joining the company."

Arjun was pleasantly surprised. He had not even anticipated his name to be there in the list so he had not paid any heed to that emailer. It took him some time to sink in.

"Savor this moment! Bask in the glory! Enjoy your success! You deserve it!"

"Thanks Harish. Couldn't have done this without you!"

"Off Course! But now you must let go of me. I shall be posted in the Regional office now. You will have a new boss!"

"That's sad. I am gonna miss you."

"But don't you worry at all! If your new boss turns out to be like Sharat, then let me know immediately. I will screw him up! That's what Regional Managers are for", Harish laughed out loud!

"Yes of course! After all that's the whole point of being near and dear to the big boss! But don't you worry. The Sharat and Devraj episode has taught me that I will find all kinds of people in my profssional journey. I must learn how to deal with them and diferent situations in life. And I can't expect someone like you to protect me always. After all you also may part ways with me sometime."

"That's right. I think I have trained you well! I am damn sure that you can handle it all by yourself. Come on now let's get to work and sell some insurance."

"Harish, I need a moment alone!"

"Sure! Go ahead!"

Arjun went out on the sprawling balcony of the office that opened up towards the entire city of Navi Mumbai. The news he had received was yet to sink in. But he was thinking about one thing and one person, Diya. He had promised her that he will be the best in what he does. And this award meant he had achieved what he had promised. He had to tell this to her immediately. He dialed her number. She didn't pick up. So he sent her a message that he had been awarded the best Sales Manager in his vertical and he had fulfilled his promise to her. After a while he received her reply.

"You did it! I am so thrilled Arjun! I have no words to say how happy I am for you. I'll call you soon. Meanwhile, enjoy your success!"

He was overjoyed to receive her message and he waited eagerly for her call back.

He got back to his work desk and opened up his email. He had another notification beeping on his laptop. But this was on his personal email Id. He was feeling overwhelmed with the turn of the events of the past couple of days. It seems it was not over yet!. That email subject line read "Letter of Appointment."

He opened the email and smiled. Immediately he rang up Saurabh and said, "Buddy, the appointment letter has arrived, finally! I got the job in the ad agency that you recommended me."

23

Letting Go

Arjun stood in front of his team at ZCP, his heart heavy with mixed emotions. Charu, Ganesh, and Rajan sat around the table in their cubicle, their faces glum, reflecting the somber mood of the moment. The usual buzz of the office seemed distant as they processed the news of him moving on.

Charu's eyes welled up with tears. "Sir, you've been an incredible mentor and friend. It's hard to imagine this place without you."

Ganesh nodded in agreement. "Sir, despite us having behaved so badly with you in the initial days, you have been so kind to us. You've always had our backs. It's going to be so different without you."

Rajan, usually the jokester, was uncharacteristically quiet. "Who's going to push us to be our best now?" he finally asked, his voice breaking slightly.

Arjun smiled, feeling a surge of affection for his team. "You all have what it takes to succeed. I've seen your potential, and I know you'll continue to excel. This isn't goodbye forever. I'll always be just a call away."

Charu wiped her eyes and managed a small smile. "We'll miss you, Sir. But we're happy for you and your new journey."

"Thank you, Charu," Arjun said, his voice warm. "And thank you all for making this journey so memorable. I couldn't have asked for a better team."

With heartfelt goodbyes and promises to keep in touch, Arjun gathered his things and took one last look around the office. As he walked out the door, he remembered his conversation with Brajesh, as he had broken the news to him earlier. He remembered each word he had said moments ago "Arjun, you have shown real character in your tenure here. Only a true professional can keep his values intact in tough times. Never lose the strength of your character. Never lose that trait of yours, ever. "

As he went outside the ZCP campus, he felt a mix of nostalgia and excitement for the future. This chapter was closing, but a new one was about to begin.

***

A couple of days after his resignation, Arjun received the long awaited call from Diya. He answered, his heart skipping a beat, unsure of what to expect.

"Hi, Arjun," Diya's voice was warm but held a tone of finality. "I wanted to tell you something important. I'm moving on in life, and... I'm going to get married."

Arjun felt a rush of emotions flood through him. His grip on the phone tightened, and for a moment, he couldn't find his voice. He had always known that Diya didn't share his feelings, but hearing her say she was getting married made it all painfully real.

"That's... that's great, Diya," he managed to say, his voice steady but tinged with sadness. "Congratulations. I hope you'll be very happy."

"Thank you, Arjun," she replied, her voice softening. "Actually, it was decided a lot earlier. But I didn't want to spoil your moment of glory. I wanted to tell you personally because I know how much our friendship means to you."

"Of course," Arjun said, trying to smile through the phone. "I wish you all the best. You deserve all the happiness in the world."

Diya changed her tone now. she sounded emapthetic. "Arjun. I know this news has devastated you. I am sorry for not making this less painful. It will tear you apart for a long time. But time would heal this. Someday this pain will be gone and what will only remain is sweet memories of the past. Remember I will always be there for you. But for now you have to let go of me. You have so much to look forwad to."

"Sure Diya! I understand. I will miss you always, " said Arjun on the brink of breaking down.

As they continued talking, Arjun realized something had changed within him. While the news hurt, it also brought a sense of closure. Diya's decision to move on was the final push he needed to let go of the past he had been clinging to. He felt a strange sense of relief, a newfound strength emerging from the sadness.

"You know, Diya," he said, his voice firmer now, "I'm excited about my new career in advertising. It's a big change, but I think it's the right move for me. It's time for me to focus on my future."

"I'm glad to hear that, Arjun," Diya said, genuinely happy for him. "You have so much potential, and I know you'll do great."

Their conversation wrapped up on a positive note, with both of them wishing each other well. As Arjun hung up, he felt a mix of emotions but primarily a sense of liberation.

Diya's news, though initially painful, had given him the push he needed to fully embrace his new life and career.

Looking out of the window, Arjun took a deep breath. He felt ready to move on, to focus on his priorities, and to embrace the opportunities ahead. Diya's call marked the end of one chapter and the beginning of another. It was time to let go, and he felt surprisingly at peace with that.

24

Exit Interview

As Arjun entered Priya's office for his exit interview, a mix of emotions washed over him. The room was brightly lit, with sunlight streaming through the large windows, casting long shadows across the polished wooden desk. Priya sat behind it, her expression a blend of professionalism and curiosity.

"Good morning, Arjun," Priya greeted, gesturing for him to take a seat.

"Good morning," Arjun replied, sitting down and trying to maintain his composure.

Priya glanced at the papers on her desk before looking back at Arjun. "So, Arjun, you've decided to move on. What prompted your decision?"

Arjun took a deep breath. "It's been a combination of things, Priya. The recent turmoil, the challenges, and honestly, the realization that I need a new environment to grow further. This place has been great, but I feel it's time for a change."

Priya nodded, taking notes. "I understand. Is there anything specific that you feel could have been done differently to make you stay?"

Arjun thought for a moment. "I think better support from management and more transparent communication and better treatment while I was a fresher could have helped."

Priya sighed. "Yes, we've had our fair share of issues recently. But I appreciate your honesty. You've been a valuable member of the team, and your contributions haven't gone unnoticed."

Arjun smiled slightly, feeling a twinge of regret. "Thank you, Priya. I've learned a lot here, and I'm grateful for the experiences."

Priya leaned forward, her tone softening. "What are your plans now, Arjun?"

Arjun hesitated for a moment before responding, "I've decided to move into the advertising industry."

Priya's eyebrows shot up in surprise. "Advertising? That's quite a shift from insurance. Why the sudden change in industry? Aren't you negating all the experience you've gained here at Zencorp?"

Arjun shrugged, a determined look in his eyes. "I understand it seems like a drastic change. But I have come to know that selling insurance is not my cup of tea."

"Arjun you were just awarded the top sales Manager in your vertical", Priya said, her tone still loaded with surprise.

"Yes Priya. But the motivation to achieve that was different. It wasn't positive. It was not to achieve something for myself, but to bring someone else down. Besides, I'm very young. This is the time for me to experiment and find my true calling. I've learned a lot here, but I want to explore different avenues and see where my passion truly lies."

Priya nodded thoughtfully, taking in his words. "I see. Well, it's good to explore while you're young. Just know that the experience you've gained here will always be valuable, no matter where you go."

"That's what I believe too," Arjun replied with a smile. "Every experience teaches you something new, and I want to make the most of my early career to gather as many diverse experiences as possible."

Priya smiled back, a hint of admiration in her eyes. "I wish you all the best, Arjun. You've got the potential to achieve great things."

As the interview wrapped up, Priya stood up and extended her hand. "Thank you for everything, Arjun. You'll be missed."

Arjun shook her hand, feeling a sense of closure. "Thank you, Priya. Thanks for the most unique experiences here. I'll miss this place too."

As he exited Priya's cabin, Priya sat back in her chair, her thoughts drifting to the events that had led to this moment. She and her husband Sharat had conspired to make Arjun's tenure at Zencorp difficult, hoping to drive him out. Yet, as she watched him leave, she realized that while their goal had been achieved, it wasn't in the way they had envisioned.

Arjun had finally resigned, but on his own terms, and this was a stark difference from what she and Sharat had planned. Instead of leaving in defeat, he was leaving with a sense of purpose and excitement for the future. Priya couldn't help but feel a pang of guilt and remorse. Here was a young professional, a fresher who had weathered the corporate storm with resilience and determination, now stepping into a new chapter of his life with confidence.

She kept her demeanor as professional as ever during their conversation. She maintained her composure, her face a mask of professionalism. But inside, her emotions were conflicted. She remembered all the subtle and not-so-subtle obstacles she and Sharat had placed in Arjun's path, hoping to see him falter. Yet, here he was, leaving on a high note, ready to explore new horizons.

As they spoke, there was an unsaid understanding between them. Both knew the undercurrents of their professional exchange. Arjun, with his quiet confidence, seemed to acknowledge her inner turmoil without a word. Priya, on the other hand, felt a strange mix of respect and regret. She had tried to knock him over, but he had risen above it all.

Their conversation had remained professional, but the silence between the words spoke volumes. Priya's thoughts were a whirlwind of guilt and reluctant admiration for Arjun's tenacity. She watched him walk away, her mind replaying the moments of their interaction, realizing that despite her intentions, Arjun had left on a high note.

As the door closed, Priya sighed softly, feeling a weight in her chest. She had achieved her goal, but it felt hollow. Arjun had survived and thrived despite the odds, and in that moment, she couldn't help but respect him. She knew she would remember this day for a long time, a day that had not gone as planned, but had revealed much about the strength of character.

Priya remained seated, lost in her thoughts, the professional veneer intact but her mind filled with introspection. Both she and Arjun had played their roles perfectly, but the outcome had left her feeling less accomplished and more reflective than she had anticipated.

Meanwhile Arjun walked out of Zencorp's head office, each step feeling lighter than the last. As he exited the building, he paused for a moment, taking in the familiar surroundings one last time. The sun was shining, and the bustling energy of the office was in full swing.

Arjun smiled to himself, feeling a newfound sense of freedom and excitement for the future. He knew that while this chapter had ended, a new and promising one awaited. With a deep breath, he stepped out into the world, ready to embrace whatever came next.

Epilogue

Arjun spent two years at the ad agency, living in Mumbai alongside Saurabh and Rishi, who remained at Zencorp. He and Diya continued to remain friends and always stayed in touch. Although Rishi apologized many times and left Arpita, Devyani never forgave him and completely broke up with him. Charu, Rajan, and Ganesh worked at Zencorp for a while before moving on individually. By the time the last of them departed, they had significantly increased the business sevenfold. Mr. Brajesh left Zencorp a year later to establish his own consultancy firm. Devraj joined another financial services company but was later accused of financial fraud and ended up in jail. Sharat faced considerable scrutiny but managed to retain his position at the company, though his influence waned. Priya left Zencorp to start her HR recruitment firm, focusing on nurturing young talent for the corporate world. She would quote incidents inspired by her experiences with Arjun as case studies for young recruits. The MD continued to lead Zencorp with unwavering vision and integrity, always on the lookout for promising new talent. He, having expanded his collection, now owned the latest models of Lexus, Jaguar, Rolls Royce, Ferrari, and a Maybach, all insured by the Zencorp team at ZCP.

ᴘᴘᴘ